I0581561

PEOPLE LIVE HERE
STORIES FROM YAKIMA

Printed in the United States of America

First Printing, 2020

Cover photo by Chris Boswell

ISBN 978-1-7365903-2-4

Simul Books
3710 SW Idaho Terrace
Portland, OR 97221

www.simulbooks.com
www.joejohnsonwrites.com

PEOPLE LIVE HERE
STORIES FROM YAKIMA

JOE JOHNSON

SIMUL
BOOKS

PORTLAND, ORE

In memory of
Angie (Morano) Noble
1973–2020

CONTENTS

FRONT MATTER

The following collection originated with stories I wrote during my studies at Central Washington University in Ellensburg, Washington, 2009–2010. My objective was to focus on aspects of a place I knew reasonably well and that produced complicated, often contradictory, feelings. Yakima was such a place. I love it, I hate it, I left it, I may be buried there.

The stories have been revisited over the years, and some have been published. I've added a few on the way. They may be decent or terrible, though I've lost all objective distance. Some make me blush, and some make me proud. As such, the best solution—rather than apologizing for errors that only bother me or editing out the qualities that make these interesting— was to simply collect them, once and for all, and present them as-is. If people love them, I take full credit. If readers find them dull, amateurish, or clumsy, I claim "student work."

The preface to this collection comes from one I drafted for the thesis, though for that project, I used something more academic. I've restored that original preface here because it provides context that might prove useful for people not familiar with the region and because it shows the era most of these stories came from. Some of the technology, geography, and language is dated. Again, I'm not going to fix that. I would have to change too many other things to make the stories match (the old saying about not putting new wine in old wineskins).

Belated thanks go to Lisa Norris, my university supervisor for many of these works. The blemishes, of course, are all mine.

PREFACE
PEOPLE LIVE HERE

The Cascade Mountains divide Washington and enforce peace between desert and forest, liberal and conservative, Cougar and Husky. They split the state like a before-and-after testimonial, with the plain farm girl set against a cosmopolitan woman, Mary Ann versus Ginger. To the outsider, the western half is Washington. It's where rain, money, and culture fall. The western half is Boeing, Bill Gates, and Bruce Lee. It's Amazon, Nirvana, and an oceanfront view. When Mount St. Helens coughed 540 million tons of ash and carcinogens, it spewed east, unwilling to tarnish the state's finest features.

Those Cascades are the regional gods, partisan and promiscuous. They mated with the waters and the plains and among themselves (as the neglected Olympic range, now separated by the Puget Sound, tries to forget). They gave birth to demigods, children of varying resemblance. In the west these children became verdant hills, favorite sons endowed with timber and wildlife. These hills held the wealth of the region: lumber, recreation, real estate. To the east, these unions produced bald protrusions speckled in sagebrush and snakes, hills useful only for rangeland until irrigation brought farming.

Yet, if water trickles past the Cascades' watch, there are moments when the eastern slopes show their heritage. If the snowpack holds in February, if the drizzle accumulates in March, if rain falls in April, those hills, even as far as Yakima, flash green. The orchards fill with blossoms and the deciduous trees look deceptively native, the hills giving the illusion of enduring beauty. In these rare moments, the traveler and the pilgrim can be convinced that Yakima, a town past the eastern slopes, herself is beautiful.

Once upon a time, it seemed that Yakima would become the capital of Washington. Had Yakima joined forces with the small rodeo town of Ellensburg, central Washington would have prevailed over the precociously-named westside town of Olympia. There's no way to say that relocation would have changed the Northwest in any meaningful way. Seattle was already on the way to becoming *Seattle!* But, perhaps decades of legislators, ambassadors, and lawyers would have infused more capital into Yakima. Maybe they and their families would have brought a greater love for the arts and deeper appreciation for higher education.

Whatever Yakima might have been, it *is* a pastiche of détentes, hidden resentments, and an ever-changing economic and real estate map. Some parts of Yakima have more in common with southern Texas than the mariner cultures along the Puget Sound. The gangs in this modest-size town rival those in larger cities such as Tacoma and Spokane. Yakima has its own claims to infamy in terms of unemployment, poverty, sexually transmitted diseases, violence, and property damage. Its downtown, once reminiscent of *Back to the Future*'s 1950s Americana, has suffered from poor business and a migrating center. Despite a strong blue-collar work base and relatively inexpensive commercial land, few industries migrate to area, and many promising immigrants, such as Delta Airlines or ClientLogic, quickly find that Yakima is a nicer place to visit than live.

But live here, people do. Many of them have lived here for generations, drawn by agriculture or Boise Cascade (now closed) or the moderate pace. They have worked in this nationally-anonymous town and watched the change in demographic, from 1900's 3,154 residents—when the state average was 99.5 percent "white"—to 71,845 in 2000, when over one third of Yakima claimed Hispanic origin. (Despite this large minority population, less than two percent of the current population is composed of members of the Yakama Nation, the city's namesake.)

The people who live here represent a host of vocations, ideologies, and incomes, united primarily by proximity. But this does not mean these populations like to talk with each other. The town is split into discernable regions: the gang-infested areas of the "Presidential streets" (Garfield, Roosevelt, and McKinley), the middle-class European housing between 24th Avenue and 40th, and the impoverished lots near the fairgrounds, to name a few. Many of the middle and upper classes have moved outside the city limits, east and west, or to the hillside fortress in the northwest corner of town. Low-income, multi-ethnic populations filled the abandoned homes.

As Los Angeles was once marked by orange groves, Yakima's borders were set by orchards: apples, pears, peaches, and hops. The first settlements were farms and fields, and these rural landowners cooperated with city-dwellers to shape a downtown. Eventually, car dealerships and chain stores followed and formed the commercial vein circulating goods and culture to the socially-segregated enclaves. As LA, Yakima is sprawling and hostile to pedestrians. And even if one were to risk being run over by unyielding cars, Yakima—unlike LA—has few destinations.

There is a glimmer of faded beauty in Yakima, like the fifty-something woman before the baggy sweatshirts, softened figure, and Liza Minnelli haircut. At one point, this was an attractive town. Some remnants of more stylish days are easy to spot: the New York-influenced Larson building, the vaudevillian-era Capitol Theater, the old brick train station. In recent years, especially following the loss of the downtown core (The Yakima Mall, JC Penney's, Nordstrom, and The Bon), significant changes have redressed the downtown. It's easy for residents to be cynical of the new-ish Hilton hotel, a glitzy, but more exclusive phoenix rising from the old Mall's ashes; it was, after all, built by a businessman many consider responsible for the Mall's closure. Still, programs like the Yakima Futures Initiative and Operation Downtown Renaissance have resuscitated areas that would have easily been left for dead. The Barrel House wine bar is a vital upgrade over the Blue Banjo, a terrifying dive that might have been paralleled in the *Star Wars* universe: "You will never find a more wretched hive of scum and villainy."

It may be too late to save Yakima if the goal is to make it something it was. The West and East Valley residents won't return to the city center. Most of the big box stores have set up shop in the neighboring town of Union Gap, the original settlement site of Yakima. Crime and poverty rates show few signs of dropping. Yet, through all these years and changes, people have moved here. They have raised families and invested in businesses and shopped along First Street. They have gone to public schools, held barbecues, played city league softball, and worked the orchards. Considering that the population has grown seventeen percent between 2000 and 2008, Yakima will remain home for many people, for several years.

The other side of the mountains, the westside—the wet side—will continue as the image Washington presents. Washington is, after all, the "Evergreen State," and Yakima's only naturally occurring green lasts a couple weeks before fading to brown. Seattle looks better on film and television. It features in movies from *Sleepless in Seattle* to *Say Anything* to *WarGames*. John Wayne even lived in the Emerald City as McQ. The *Twilight* vampires stayed in a corner of Washington as far from Yakima as possible. The last, and perhaps only, movie to feature Yakima was *Extreme Days*, an Evangelical-funded film about extreme sports teens, which grossed less than $2 million and didn't show a single frame of the town.

But there are still stories here. A few of these are in this collection, based on events and people in Yakima. These are influenced by the tone and texture that soak into a writer's imagination from living in a place. In any case, the point of writing about Yakima is describing life, much as it is when writing about Dublin, New York, or Paris. It's about asking how a place and a people blend until the city and the citizen— like the old cliché about a pet and its master—begin to resemble one another. This group of short stories is simply a collection of snapshots and vignettes that try to show the relationship between character and context. In this case, that context is a place few people will ever visit, and fewer still will ever claim as home. But still, people live here. (2010)

STARLINGS
84TH AVE AND TIETON

"I'm not prejudice or anything," Mr. Woods says. Like I believe him. "It's just the Mexicans. The ones here illegally, I mean. There's lots of 'em who came here the right way. The other Mexicans. They're killing the place."

I nod. I don't mean it. And since we're alone in Mr. Woods's kitchen, colleagues and Chicanos will never know my complicit racism. Nodding is the polite thing to do. It's a tactic.

Mr. Woods is massive. It doesn't matter that I'm aware of the legal definition of "assault." The man is a bear, a beast with arms that could fell trees. And he's the law in this kitchen. I try to concentrate on the signs of weakness: the ring of receded gray-blond hair, the shabby denim overalls, the waxy skin. This man's as old as my grandfather, and Grandpa wheezes walking to the bathroom.

"It's the government and how it pays them to come up here," he says. "They just keep taking from hardworking Americans."

"The government or the Mexicans?"

"Both." He pauses. "Yeah, both. The government—it just keeps taking money—wants Mexicans to come here so there's something to spend money on, something for the government to raise taxes for. And the Mexicans—hell, I don't blame 'em— they come up here to get it. They put their kids in school and they don't even speak English. And we pay for that, too. Then they make us say sorry because we don't speak Spanish. Lo siento."

I'm nodding again. Adult men shouldn't be this spineless. I'm nodding, agreeing, with this old farmer—this balding, bumbling man who gets his politics from talk radio on a tractor.

"One of these days, the Mexicans are gonna want more. They're gonna ask for my trucks or the orchard or the house, and the government will just say, 'Take it, señor. Anything else you want? Anything else taxpayers can give you?'"

"Do you really think that?"

His bottom lip drops. Woods points out the window at the trees. "When my granddad grew this orchard, kids like me picked everything. Hell, the day I finished third grade, my dad had me out here. First cherries, then apples. We worked all summer. And not just me. It was my friends at school. That's just how it was. No one complained about it, and there's no one saying things should be this way or that way. It was just life."

I try to imagine *boy* Carl Woods scaling ladders, pocketing the biggest cherries for himself. Boy Carl wears the same overalls, has the same gut: only the hair, a bush of summer-blond hair, and the scale differ.

"My dad said things changed with the Mexicans. He said if we weren't careful, one of the Mexicans would fall off a ladder and then some college kid from Seattle, who came here to make a name for himself, that college kid'd sue us. Take the whole farm. Maybe some kid like you. Would you do that?"

I stop nodding. "Did that ever happen?"

"Might as well. Now all the pickers are Mexicans and all the foremen are Mexicans, and my grandson grew up with all the Mexican kids. Who knows if they're legal or not? I'd get arrested just asking. Between the girls and his phone, my boy's kid isn't good for farming. He just wants to play video games and text or email or whatever garbage he does on that phone. Now the Mexicans are the only ones who even want the farm anymore."

"Ironic?"

"What?"

"Ironic. Strange turn of events," I say. "Maybe you have more in common with the Mexicans than you do with your own son."

"*Grandson*. My son's dead. It's my grandson. We've been raisin' him since my boy died."

"I'm sorry for your loss," I say.

"And I know what irony is," says Woods. "I went to college. I read Hemingway and Steinbeck and that other guy—the one who wrote about Mississippi."

"Faulkner?"

"Faulkner. Twain, too. So I get irony. And, no," he says, "it's not ironic. It's not funny. It's just the way of the world. Hell, my granddad always thought Jesus would return before the world got like this."

The table top is two inches of worn white oak. I rub my hands across it, wishing for it to transfer wisdom, telling me what words to use. It gives me nothing. I'm left with, "Mr. Woods, you know why I'm here, right?"

"Carl," he says.

"Carl?"

"Call me Carl." He rises from his chair, walks to the orange-crème Formica counter, pours coffee. "You sure you don't want any? It's good. Not the Starbuck stuff—if you can stomach that sugar water. This is real coffee."

"No, thanks."

"Suit yourself."

The percolating glass-bulb coffee pot, the doilies, the "icebox" belong to another time. Woods himself, with his Teddy Roosevelt mustache, is a walking relic worthy of a museum. The display plaque would read, "Lone-American Gothic."

"I know why you're here," he says.

"You do?"

"And I think it's a waste of everyone's time. A sin, maybe," he says. "This land belongs to us, and it needs to be farmed. God designed it to be farmed. He took out the rocks. He gave us the sun and the river. It's all meant to be farmed, and, believe it or not, I'd rather have trucks stuffed with illegals driving cross this land, jumping through my family's trees, than socialist liberals plowing it to the ground and covering it with concrete." He sips his coffee. "No offense."

I wave my hand across my chest, shake my head. "None taken," I say.

"This is orchard land. It grows. Putting up houses or a McDonald's or some shopping center—or whatever you folks want to do with it—ain't good and ain't gonna' happen if I can stop it."

I consider quoting Joni Mitchell, but I doubt Woods will accept sympathy from a Canadian folk singer. Instead, I say, "So, we're at an impasse?"

"You could say that."

"And there's nothing I can do to change your mind."

"Can't think of anything."

"This isn't a threat," I say. "I'm not going to try any hard sell, but you know it's a matter of time. The Thompsons sold. The Shrivers sold. In five years, your orchard will be an island."

"My orchard's already an island, Mr. Beckley."

"Steven," I say.

"Alright. My orchard's already an island, Steven. And I'm an island. I don't care what some poet says—a man can be an island. But the island's all I got. There's lots of islands like mine. Most of us islands know where the others are, too."

I wish I had recorded this. "Do you mean a network, like a militia?"

Something like a smile settles beneath Woods's mustache. "For all your school you don't know much." Woods pulls out his chair and sits then leans over the table so we're almost eye level. "I know what you're thinking. You're saying in your head, 'This Woods guy, he's got a bomb shelter and three years' worth of beans and ammunition.' I know those people. Maybe they got a point. Maybe they're just like Jefferson and Revere and all those men who fought for this country. But that's not what I'm talking about." He sips. "I don't think you'd get it if I told you."

I hadn't thought him the bomb shelter kind. But now I envision books about the Rapture, Jesus returning in the clouds and planes falling from the sky. Maybe Carl Woods hides gold bars across his farm. Maybe he has an arsenal of unregistered automatic weapons.

"Mr. Woods," I say.

"Carl."

"Carl," I say. "I don't think any of those things, and even if I did—even if they were true—that doesn't mean anything to me. I figure, as long as the law says it's fine to keep a shelter and weapons, then what business of it is mine, right?"

"It is your business Mr. Beckley."

"Steven."

"All of this is your business, Steven. It's your business to care about this country or this land, or what happens to this land if I'm not on it. You see, we grow food here." He squeezes his mug as he says this, like he's juicing it. "When you put an Olive Garden or a Taco Bell where this orchard is, well, you got a problem. See that restaurant doesn't have any food if you don't have orchards and farms. Food isn't something you can make without land, and if you take this land, you take the food. Now, I may not be sensitive. Hell, I may not be a person you like much—"

"I think you're a good man."

"And I think you're a bad liar. But that don't matter. You think you're not doing any harm." He stands, lifting his arms. He's a grizzly about to swipe a salmon.

"You ever grow food?" he says. "You ever plant something, pray over it, watch it come out of the dirt? You ever water it, trim it back, set oil lanterns at three in the morning so it don't get too cold?"

I shrug.

"I do that. I beg God for snow in the winter and sun in the summer. I do that so folks like you can have cherries when they want 'em. And I'm glad people like cherries. The more cherries you put in your ice cream, the better. We put nets up and tinsel and we chase away birds—those damned starlings. Sometimes, I pull out my .22 and I shoot at those birds. Of course that bothers some people. Probably bothers you."

He knows it does.

"Those people say, 'Oh, how can you shoot at starlings?' And

I just tell 'em, 'Starlings don't belong here, and farmers know that it comes down to starlings or cherries.'"

"Birds don't belong on trees?"

"Not *birds*, Mr. Beckley. Starlings."

"What's the difference?"

"You take any Shakespeare at college?"

"A semester."

"You don't know about starlings?"

"I know what starlings are."

"That's not what I mean. See, starlings don't belong here. They're immigrants, brought here by Shakespeare-lovers in England. They thought, 'Shakespeare talks about starlings and starlings are so pretty, we ought to bring 'em to America.'"

"Is that true?"

"And that's what you are—and the folks you work for," he says. "And that's what these other folks around here are."

"I'm a starling?"

"Yes, you're a starling. You're a bird that flies in here and you see my trees and you think, 'I'm gonna swing down there and get the fruit I didn't plant, the fruit I didn't warm or keep dry. I'm just gonna fly down there and poke at those cherries and get drunk on 'em and not pay anything.' And then you think, once you're all full, 'Now I'll fly off and look for more cherries.'"

I think people are, generally, reasonable and deserve understanding. Most people, like the Thompsons and the Shrivers, see change coming and they don't like it, but they know it's coming and it's nobody's fault. But Woods thinks it's my fault. He thinks there's a conspiracy and that we're all in on it: me, Starbucks, the government, the Mexicans, the birds.

"You sure you don't want some coffee?" Woods says. He lifts

the tin kettle before staring back out his window.

"No, Mr. Woods, I think I've taken enough of your time." I reach down, grab my attaché, the one with a laptop and a contract waiting for a signature that won't come. Not from Carl Woods.

Woods walks ahead of me. He twists the old door knob, some brass and glass fixture I only ever see in these old houses.

"You tell your bosses you tried, but there isn't anything they got that I want."

"I'll tell them that," I say. I reach out my hand. Woods envelops it with his paw. I'm eight again, shaking hands with my father, with some form of masculinity that I never became.

"Goodbye, Mr. Woods," I say.

"Carl," He says.

"Carl," I say.

I don't care much for Carl Woods, but I almost feel sorry for him: the dryness of his voice, the black around his eyes. He's fighting something he can't beat. In a few years, two at the most, he won't be able to work his orchard. In three, it will be in his grandson's hands, and that kid will sell. He won't see it as an orchard or a history or a trust. He'll see the investment, the cash. He'll be reasonable, and he'll trade Carl Woods's orchard for freedom. He'll fly away and never see these trees again.

ARRIVALS AND DEPARTURES
33RD AVE AND ENGLEWOOD

The nurse tapped, one knuckle, on Miriam's door. She entered without waiting for an invitation. "The van's here," she said. She smiled as she said this. She smiled the way every nurse, every custodian, and every intern at Palm Community smiled—as if to say, "We can't wait until we get to live here. It's happy here. It's a happy place to be old. You're so lucky to be old." The old smiled sometimes, too. Usually when remembering.

Miriam was smiling before the knock. She had been rubbing her thumb against the pewter frame. The picture of Tom, her beloved.

Miriam straightened her face. She returned Tom to the desk and massaged her hands. These hands had been strong once and useful.

Miriam was not alone in the van. Harvey and Richard, both wearing stiff, black, insignia-laced baseball caps, filled the first two seats. Harvey's old service jacket, speckled with patches and ribbons. Richard's blue vest, decorated like a Boy Scout's. The driver closed the double-door as Miriam waddled to her seat. The driver wrote some notes on a small pad. He buckled himself.

The plane would come—the P-38 Lockheed Lightning, two planes joined as one—a plane that had not flown since the War. It was the plane, or its twin, Tom piloted over the Bismarck Sea fighting the Japanese at New Guinea. One of those planes, and maybe Tom had known it, would land here, in Yakima, in a town hidden from war, far from Japan and New Guinea.

Harvey and Richard reminisced of Roosevelt and MacArthur and Midway. The last half-century never happened. There was no Watergate or computer age. No Clinton impeachment or Hurricane Katrina. There was only the War and the Draft, the assurance that the United States needed their service. Their service had saved the world from tyranny. They were the greatest among the greatest generation.

Harvey described the P-38s he maintained when stationed in England. He fought against Rommel when the unit moved to Africa. Richard romanced about the Pacific and bringing down Yamamoto on the way to Bougainville Island. He recalled shaking hands with Jimmy Doolittle. "And you know the movie they made about him," he said. "General Doolittle didn't look anything like Spencer Tracy."

Miriam wanted to believe them. She wanted to believe the War was still on and that these men, men like Tom, were still vital and relevant. But she could only think of Dr. Dyer. "The atoms in the human body change every seven years," he said. The airmen that fought those wars had been recycled nine times. Miriam's own body had changed four times since retiring from teaching, three times since becoming a great grandmother, twice since Tom died. Dr. Dyer couldn't explain why her body never changed for the better. "That's just how it works," he said. "So watch the sodium."

Miriam tried to focus on the houses blurring by. Most seemed alien. A few were shells of homes she once knew. One had belonged to her sister. Janet would have fainted seeing the cars on her lawn, on the brittle, brown grass her dear George had nurtured for thirty-five years. It was God's good mercy that neither George nor Janet had lived to see such indifference.

For Miriam, the ride from Palm Community to the airport was like her European train tour with Tom, the retirement/ anniversary trip: Miriam glued to the windows, watching the houses for five hours, Innsbruck to Florence. The architecture never changed. The same steepled roofs and wood balconies lined the tracks from southern Austria to northern Italy. But with each kilometer south, the buildings aged. "Do you see this, dear?" she asked. "It's the same house over and over again, but it gets more run down the closer we get to Rome." Tom was reading. As Italy passed by, Tom was in Durango with Louis L'Amour.

Miriam hadn't been to the airport since Tom died. They used to go to the annual airshow, when there was one, and she would follow Tom, watching him point and dash, listening to him tell stories. Tom knew every plane built before 1962 and how it served in the Pacific, in Korea, in Vietnam. He was a boy then, even as his skin lost elasticity, as his freckles seemed to pool, like tan drops of mercury, into spots.

The airport was much as Miriam remembered: the parking lot resembling a cattle ranch with cars crammed like livestock, belly to belly. The terminal itself could have been an old highway motel stretched across half a block. It was plain and white, with a second story tacked on and a lone lighthouse tower to the east. Matching white buildings and hangers ran the perimeter. Miriam didn't remember what they were for. Tom used to know.

The van parked curbside at one of the spots that doubled

for arrivals and departures. The driver unbuckled, levered open the doors, stepped out, and opened the specialized ramp door on Miriam's side of the bus. Neither Miriam nor the old veterans needed wheelchairs. Still, each of them struggled to stand. Harvey whimpered and grabbed his upper thigh. Richard rocked his torso, gripped the driver's seat in front, and pulled himself up. The veterans braced themselves as Miriam flexed the remaining muscles in her legs and pulled against a bar to rise. The men waited for her—perhaps from an anachronistic chivalry, perhaps out of the shame of having to limp to the sidewalk.

Apart from superficial changes—new rental car companies, new colored uniforms, flat panel computer screens—the interior was as Miriam and Tom had left it. The check-in counters were to her right. The baggage claim to her left. The terminals were directly ahead. She and Tom would sometimes spend mornings in the terminals—Tom with his coffee and she with a blueberry muffin—watching flights come in and talking about places they should visit. During one of those mornings, they decided to tour Italy.

The terminal entrances, though, were peculiar. They were gated and guarded by uniformed men and glass walls, like embassies or secrets. According to the news channels and government pronouncements, according to the warnings on the flat screen TVs, these barriers were for Miriam and her safety.

At Palm Community, Miriam passed her days watching news reports. She listened to the radio. She believed every commentator and pundit insisting on the need to protect borders and catch terrorists. But the danger was in New York and Afghanistan. The danger was olive-skinned Muslims with red eyes and venom sent by Mohammad to kill American Christians. That war was about foreigners and metropolises, places and people far from Yakima. Far from orchards and little Baptist churches and the Palm Community Assisted Living Center.

Miriam leaned against a wall in the waiting area as Harvey and Richard lumbered toward the new gates. Harvey showed his pass to one of the uniformed guards. The guard shook his head. Harvey cupped his ear. The guard spoke again, and the old man nodded. Harvey removed his jacket and placed it on a pink tray, which was then set on a conveyer belt. The jacket medals were x-rayed. Harvey walked through a beige portal and set off a red light and a metallic buzz.

A guard flashed his palm, stopping Harvey from going farther. He mouthed something. He gestured to the entry side of the gate. Harvey looped for a second pass. Another guard closed in on the old vet and pointed to a chair. Harvey eased into the seat and unlaced his shoes. He placed them on another pink tray. The first guard set the tray on the conveyor belt as the second ushered Harvey through the detector. The red signal lit. The buzzer sounded.

A pudgy Hispanic woman in a blue uniform approached Harvey. She held a white plastic wand and scanned it over his body in the event he might be hiding something. The medals and insignia of Harvey's cap frightened the wand, so Harvey set his hat on another pink tray. He returned through the portal. This time, it allowed him to pass.

Behind Harvey, the second guard—a short, stocky man with a barbwire tattoo on his wrist—asked Richard to follow him.

Miriam could hear fragments.

—"We apologize, sir."

—"Policy."

—"I understand. But we check everyone. It's our duty."

Richard removed his coat, then his shirt, and set them in a gray basin. He stripped to a loose white undershirt and stood with his arms outstretched. The guard scanned a wand over him, never losing sight of Richard's arms, as if, at any moment, the old vet might drop his hands to a detonator. The guard waved the wand over the buckle Richard bought on a Normandy reunion tour. He directed Richard to turn around. He moved the wand across Richard's backside, hovering again around the belt. He handed the basin to Richard and pointed to a set of chairs as Richard marched away, still a soldier, and dressed again.

Richard rejoined Harvey, both men emptied of war stories. They stood near other Richards and Harveys, the remaining units of sailors, soldiers, and airmen still loyal to Nimitz, Marshall, and Arnold.

Miriam stepped away from her supporting wall and lowered into one of the vinyl-leather black suspension seats. She had stopped breathing, for a moment. This airport and this town were Rome—they might as well have been. Miriam was sitting in a station, looking at foreigners. The airport belonged to another time and place, one owned by others. Miriam recognized none of these people, except Harvey and Richard. But she didn't really know them or want to know them. They were joined only because they lived and expired in the same moment. They were tourists from the same country who chanced upon one another in a foreign land. Not friends.

Not family. Accidental countrymen.

She squinted, attempting to focus past the guards and gate. She could see enough of the field from her seat to watch the P-38 come in. She was close enough. She didn't need to be closer.

GRAVEYARD
16TH AVE AND FRUITVALE

Tino parked in his usual spot, left of the dumpster. He reached to the passenger-side seat, grabbed a crumpled T-shirt, and wiped his forehead. He promised himself that, next paycheck, he would get the AC fixed. In the meantime, he could hide inside The Mart.

The Mart was a monument to 1960s industrial architecture and the capitalist imagination. Its paint strata hold the transitions from Circle K to 7-Eleven to AM/PM. It had been John's Eat'n'Seat then Jiffy's Conoco and, for a few months in the mid-90s, Wayne's Kwik Stop. But now the little convenience store, a hybrid of the great old-west traditions of general stores and saloons, had reached its essence.

The Mart greeted Tino with an electronic two-tone *dingdong* and the aroma of overwarmed corndogs. It fed Tino with free Slushees and expired chicken burgers. In return, Tino Mendoza served it, following the path of the hundreds before him who wore the orange and blue smock.

Tino kept floors, cases, and vending units clean. He directed customers to merchandise and watched the store while most of Yakima slept. He knew the store's anatomy: the Emergency Fix-A-Flat on Aisle One, the Enfamil on Six, the Chick-O-Sticks on Four (beneath the Twizzlers). He knew the machines, when to change the cheese and toss the hotdogs, how to load the syrup in the fountains. After only five months, he was third in seniority, just behind Mary, the store manager, and Diane.

Diane, the sixty-something fascist. Diane, with her gray piano-wire ear hair. Diane, with her corn kernel teeth (where she still had teeth). Diane beckoned Tino with her skeletal forefinger—her eerily accurate reenactment of the Wicked Witch poking toward Dorothy. Tino set down the promotional *Iron Man* candy straws and walked to the counter. He stood on the customer side, obscuring the *Times*, *Sports Illustrated*, and *Maxims*. Diane, the senior tyrant, waved her arm, and Tino—knowing that dachshunds were the only beings who respected Diane—interpreted the motion as the woman's command to come service-side.

"These are new forms from Mary," she said. "They are *very*—" Diane's dry tongue chafed across her chapped lips as she stressed how *very* these forms were, "—important and Mary told me to tell you that they are *very* important." All employees, Diane explained, had to track cleaning time: when and where they mopped, when they cleaned the bathroom, when they bleached the cutlery. "Mary said we have to do this. So make sure you do it."

Tino nodded.

"It's *very* important." She pointed to a picture of a mop on the form. "What does this say?"

"Mopped bathroom."

"Right. Be sure to mop the bathroom and mark the time on Mary's form."

"I'll mark everything," he said.

Diane explained how she single-handedly saved The Mart from ruin. She detailed the rush at 8:30 and the run on sausage and pizza pockets by an early lunch crowd. She told Tino Pump

Three ran out of register tape, but she heroically changed it while keeping the barbecue burritos from overcooking ("If they overcook, you might as well toss 'em out. Mary doesn't like that."). She said the coffee was fresh and that she changed chili and cheese right before Tino's shift. She emptied the inside trash cans, but the fuel-side trash still needed collecting and dumping.

"Remember—" She locked her glaucoma-ridden eyes on Tino, the community college-drop out young enough to be her grandson, and rattled like a drill sergeant: "Toss the hot dogs at midnight and make just a small pack until the morning. Close the beer case at 2:00." She enveloped Tino in her perfume of mustard and dairy creamer. "Mop the bathroom and back aisles. And use the right soap this time. I do not want to clean up after you again. Write everything on Mary's new forms. They are very important. Make new coffee at 5:00. Start the breakfast burritos at 5:15." She tried to stand erect, but her hunchback resisted. She had the curve of a cobra. She hissed as she spoke. "Sssso. Sssshouldn't you be sssstarting?"

"Right after you check out," said Tino.

"I still have to inventory the cooler," she said. "Mary asked me to do that, and I better have it finished before she gets here in the morning."

"I can do it. Mondays are dead anyway."

Diane let out a wet wheeze: her nicotined, bronchial attempt at laughter. "It's best if I do it."

"It's no problem," said Tino. "It's just inventory."

"I promised Mary I would do it. Mary likes it done right."

Tino's feet joined together, his back straightened, but he did not salute.

11:06 P.M.

Tino unwrapped a batch of sausage and cheese biscuits, loaded them onto a cooking sheet, and set the convection/ microwave/combo oven for Auto-Cook-Level-Four. By 5:30, in time for his breakfast, he could mark them for discard. He could say they had been under the lamp too long and needed to be tossed. Mary didn't check the trash, only the food sheet.

Three gamers entered. Tino knew the type. He was the type. He knew the rush of networking Xboxes and talking to strangers in Ohio and Oregon and forming internet allegiances. He had killed thousands of enemy aliens. He had watched battalions of virtual comrades fall in the effort to liberate humanity from The Covenant. Perhaps the tall guy, the blond kid with the *Halo* T-shirt, was one of them. Maybe they had met in battle before. Brothers in arms—together with Halo Shirt's two companions: Yellow Converse and Mullet.

The trio seemed able warriors, barely bloodshot from what was probably already a six-hour day, taking a break before the graveyard shift. They moved in formation to the back fridge and grabbed Dr. Peppers. Halo Shirt shouted to Mullet, "Check it. They got Jolt."

They hovered through Aisle Four, grabbed Mike and Ikes, Jambas, and Jolly Ranchers. Then Aisle Five, returning with Cool Ranch Doritos, Fun-Yuns, and Tim's Salt and Vinegar chips. Then the front counter, scanning the glass case for final spoils. Halo Shirt got two Big Dogs. Yellow Converse took a pizza pocket, chicken sandwich, and—Tino's favorite—the cheese burrito. Mullet was as picky as those westside moms who pull out a display case of milk to reach the freshest carton.

"You got any of those sausage and cheese biscuits?"

"In the oven," said Tino.

"Dude," said Halo Shirt. "Just get the taquitos."

"Three jalapeño and bacon," said Yellow Converse.

Tino gave each of them drink carriers. He considered warning them of the dangers of a mini-mart diet, how after high school the belly retains the carbs and polyhydrated shortenings and processed corn byproducts. The belly swells from thirty inches to thirty-nine. These warriors were still young and fit enough to be part of a real military, but not if they kept drilling against video invaders at midnight on Mondays. Not if they dined at The Mart.

11:51 P.M.

Tino forgot about Diane. She had been in the cooler, rearranging drinks, checking expiration dates, fronting labels so that "Coke" would jump at the customer—as if an inspector from corporate headquarters in Atlanta would come to some barely-on-the-map, central-Washington-State desert town and commend her for excellent marketing. Diane returned to the counter, carrying broken-down boxes and a clipboard. The door behind her closed with a click as it formed a sealed, environmentally controlled chamber. Diane set the clipboard on the counter and took the boxes to the dumpster.

Her signature was hideous, a strict and inartistic collection of printed letters. It was as if she had stopped writing when she was six, assuming she would never need a signature. "Inventory is done," she said. "I just have to mop the candy aisle and clean the food prep, and I'll go."

Maybe Diane was seventy, eighty. The cooler bleached

her already pale skin, making the little touches of blush and lipstick more vivid and comic. Her hair never moved. This was how she would look in a coffin.

"I can do all that," said Tino. "It's no problem."

"I promised Mary I would do it. The swing shift was busy, not like graveyard. I need to finish."

"You can tell Mary you did it for all I care."

"It's my responsibility. There's a right way to do it." Diane picked up the clipboard. Tino debated telling her the Sprite numbers were under "Dairy," that the Budweiser count was under "Lunchmeat." The last time he pointed out her mistakes, Diane ranted that he didn't understand anything, how Mary liked it the way she did it, and that maybe, *if he were around for three years*, he would know how things worked. Tino always suspected she was keeping him away from the swing shift and her seniority. She was second in charge, and maybe that kind of honor only comes with staying too late, working too hard, and exchanging the last days of life to hear a twenty-six-year-old manager, say, "Good job, Diane."

Diane filled the yellow-wheeled mop bucket with orange goo and hot water. She crouched and pulled the bucket, shuffling backwards toward the candy. She stopped by Tino, stood, and massaged the small of her back. "It's time to change the hot dogs," she said.

For all her eagerness, Diane was a poor worker. She sloshed soapy water onto the cupboards and missed patches of dried relish. Tino shot mental photos of the places he would need to fix. The Mart deserved better.

12:13 A.M.

If Tino ever took Diane's swing shift, it would be to avoid Ruby. She was pretty once. Recently, perhaps. But now she was a gypsy, always dressed in a floor-length skirt. Tonight the skirt was black with maroon and silver paisley. Ruby wore a silver polyester (too shimmery and plastic to be silk) arm-length blouse, which was covered in broaches and faux-gold chains and plastic pearl necklaces. And the scarf. Always, the scarf. Even now in late June, the ruby-red scarf. It covered some secret, some clue to her life, some key to her unending thirst. Perhaps she had a scar or a rope burn, or maybe she was simply vain, obscuring loosening skin.

Ruby wandered Aisle Three studying the canned meats. She picked up a tin of sardines. She roamed Five and fondled a box of macaroni and cheese, then a box of Cheerios. She wanted Aisle Four, but Diane was still there, still mopping, still drowning the linoleum. The senior bully made a last squeeze of the mop. She set out the orange caution cones and walked the bucket back to the storeroom.

Ruby set down a bag of pretzels and walked, without sound, to the candy aisle. Tino had seen this fifty times. He wondered how often The Mart had witnessed this. If only the store could tell him what to do. There was nothing in the employee handbook.

Ruby paused before the shelves. To an outsider, she might look like she were deciding. But she already knew. She always knew. It wasn't a question of what to get, only what flavor—and that didn't really matter. Tino figured she never ate the candy, though he imagined each flavor as a mood ring. Cherry is red, angry. Sour apple is green, worried.

Ruby set a banana Laffy Taffy on Tino's counter (yellow, distracted). It was a small, inch-wide block of hydrogenated cottonseed oil manipulated into gooeyness, transformed into unnatural color, and saturated with extra-banana-flavored banana. If Ruby opened it, she would find a joke on the wrapper. ("Why was Cinderella late for the ball?" it would ask, like the second grader that, maybe, Ruby had once been. "She forgot to swing the bat!")

She reached into her pocket, never lifting her eyes above Tino's torso. There was no energy in her motion, only obedience. She drew out the Quest card, an upgrade from the old food stamps' toy-money-like paper bills. Still, there were rules for the card. If a customer bought a Big Thirst and didn't put a straw in it, the purchase counted as food. With the straw, it was processed—a service item—and required cash.

Tino rung up the dime candy as Ruby swiped her card and entered her PIN. She was a drone. She just went about the process, the humiliating act of turning food into money and money into nectar. She opted for the twenty-dollar cash back option. Tino paused. He stared at the twenty on his register, then confirmed. His till drawer opened, and he pulled two tens. Tino handed her the change and Ruby pocketed the candy.

Ruby turned. She walked back toward the Laffy Taffy, then passed them and arrived at the line of refrigerated beverages. She opened Door Six. The filtered, nearly-frozen air poured out as Ruby grabbed a bottle from the rack. She walked back to the counter, set a strawberry-flavored-screw-top wine on it, and gave one of her tens to Tino. Tino scanned the bottle, collected the bill, and returned Ruby's change.

"Do you want a bag?"

Ruby shook her head.

"Do you want a hot dog?" he asked.

She paused.

"No charge," he said. "I was supposed to dump them at midnight."

Ruby nodded. Tino grabbed two hot dogs with buns. He also took a chicken sandwich—the one he planned to eat after Diane left—and a cheeseburger and put them into a plastic bag. He handed them to Ruby. She nodded again, and her eyes, if only for an impossibly short moment, rose to Tino's. Tino saw lost beauty and terror and gratitude and despair. He couldn't speak. He couldn't say *have a nice night* or *thank you for shopping at The Mart.* He couldn't tell her that she could come home with him. Ruby left, and the bell didn't even ring. Maybe she was a ghost. Maybe she was an angel testing him.

"Did you give twenty back on a Quest?" said Diane, with her crackled wraith voice. She closed in, armed with a spray bottle and a white cotton rag. "The store limit on those cards is five dollars cash back," she said. "Food stamps were better. You could never give anything back besides coins. When I used to work at the Conoco, if some drunk bought a piece of licorice with a ten-dollar food stamp, I'd hand back three quarters—and nine dollars in stamps. They'd just go back and forth to the candy aisle. They'd leave the store with a bottle of wine and seven Snickers."

The Slushee machine spit out a chunk of green ice.

"Damn thing," she said. "I've fixed it a hundred times."

"I think you made it spew," said Tino.

"What?"

Tino said nothing.

Diane vanished again, as quickly as she had appeared, hidden in one of the secret coolers or bathrooms or dumpsters.

1:11 A.M.

Tino embraced the solitude, almost forgetting that Diane still lurked. This peace vanished with the oboe squeak of Diane's last barrage of commands. "Don't forget to lock the case at 2:00. We get fined if you don't, and Mary will fire you. I've seen it happen." She walked to the customer side of the counter and restacked the Never-Sleep caffeine supplements. "Make sure to get a fresh pot of coffee started at 5:30. The store will be full by 6:00."

Thus ended Diane's official orders.

Diane pulled a wrinkled, slightly damp, five-dollar bill from her pocket. She pointed to a pack of menthol GPCs, the generics. On special. She mumbled "goodnight" to Tino, reminded him to mop the bathroom, and walked outside. She stood on the sidewalk outside the doors, twenty-five feet from the entrance, *per* state regulation, and lit a cigarette. She was quiet. Calm.

The wall of glass separating Diane from The Mart's interior made her almost pitiable, like a zoo's spotted hyena, captive a continent away from its home. Even her rigid wig softened with each drag. She stared out onto Fruitvale Boulevard, peaceful as a mother sipping tea after her children are tucked in. She flicked the last ember of tobacco into an empty Mountain Dew can. She put the cigarette stub in her pocket, unwilling to litter her own home.

Diane walked to the first fuel aisle and picked up a balled

and discarded paper towel. She straightened the washing blade handles, redistributing them to one per basin. She tossed the paper towel and turned back to The Mart, now, from the parking lot, a glowing enclave in a sleeping town. It wasn't Diane's fault. She was a moth.

The doors opened and the ringer sounded with a single *ding*.

"Tino. You haven't dumped the fuel-side garbage yet."

Tino faced the fragile, spiritless figure before him. Diane was smaller somehow, or perhaps thinner—like one of those hollow chocolate Easter bunnies left in the sun. Tino blinked twice before speaking, wanting to throw a tantrum but finding the strength to say—with the sort of courteous and polite smile refined by waiters and hotel clerks—"Thank you for reminding me. I always do that at 2:00 after locking the case."

"Well, it's slow enough now. You should probably get it done while you can," said Diane. "You never know when a rush will come."

Tino nodded. Diane turned and, as dully as she entered, disappeared into the night.

1:58 A.M.

Olde English made it just in time. Another two minutes and he would have had the confrontation. Tino would have to say:

—"You have to come back at 6:00."

—"It's state law."

—"No, I can't make an exception."

—"Yes, it's possible that the clock is a few minutes fast, but it's synced to the camera and my boss checks every morning. She'll fire me. I've seen it done."

The man was crippled but punctual. He was the kind who

didn't know—and wouldn't believe—that a black man was ever President, but his chemical clock always knew the time. It always sounded the alarm to get out of his chair, to stop watching *Cheers* re-runs and get to the cooler before 2:00. Even though it was summer, he couldn't take the sidewalks for granted. He had to allow time for crossing the street, for avoiding any roaming gangs, for forgetting his wallet and turning around. Something big must have slowed him, because he never risked coming this near closing.

He always bought the same 40-ounce bottle. Every shift. He never experimented with Colt 45 or Country Club. Always Olde English. Always one bottle. He wore the same corduroy brown jacket, the same brown boat shoes, like an exile from Jimmy Buffett's Margaritaville. He always traveled Aisle Five and fumbled for his wallet as he approached Tino. He always gave a full, mucus-filled smoker's cough four feet from the counter. He always had exact change.

Tino no longer talked to the man. There was no point. Olde English never responded, never acknowledged. Tino was a vending machine with a nametag.

After Olde English: a waitress finishing her shift at Denny's, two line cooks trying to get beer, and a drunk that needed Spam and a pack of Newports.

3:23 A.M.

Tino filled a Slushee but couldn't force it down. He walked the aisles, looking for messes or some amazing piece of merchandise he hadn't seen before. He checked the locks on the liquor cases. He tried singing with the barely audible musak, hoping to redeem an offensively tame version of "Smells Like

Teen Spirit."

Tino moved behind the counter and stared at the black rack. He scanned the store, as if his mother or a priest were hiding behind the baby food. He crouched. He grabbed a plastic-wrapped magazine and slit the top with a box knife. He thumbed through the *Penthouse*. It did nothing for him. He browsed an edition of *Cherry* and debated pocketing the complementary DVD. He even attempted to read an article in *Playboy*, an interview with Justin Timberlake, before the words turned into a meaningless mash of typefaces. He was a professional insomniac. He mopped the bathroom then checked it off Mary's form.

4:08 A.M.

Tino walked to the fuel islands. The air was cool, and a sliver of the moon held above the fluorescent road signs. If Tino could get away from the streetlights, maybe he could see a star. He stood outside the doors like the Omega Man searching for signs of other humans. The bee-like buzz of cars rang behind him, the early-morning motorists moving along Highway 12. He wondered if there were any commuters, any people making a trek to King County or the Tri-Cities. A gray Subaru slowed at the intersection, approaching the flashing red light but never stopping, unaware or uncaring that Tino was watching.

Tino treasured the frozen time. He found comfort in knowing that most of the town slept. This was the best part of the shift: the quiet, the stillness, the sense of being in another world.

In high school, Tino had read sections from *Travels with Charlie*, John Steinbeck's travelogue of vanishing Americana.

Sometimes Tino imagined Fruitvale Boulevard being a highway from Steinbeck's journals. It looked like lost glory, like a river diverted into a brook—a park with chain-link swings and seesaws. Perhaps life flowed along this channel in the past, but it had become a disparate smattering of niche businesses and factory storage sites. Car dealerships. Specialty shops. A Masada Shrine. Houses blended with commercial properties behind the deteriorating sidewalks. The houses visible from the road were small and broken, but they were improvements over the dens of manufactured homes and trailers buried further back. Fruitvale was once the great northern border until Highway 12 merged with the freeway and siphoned away all but the hill dwellers driving east to the Red Lobster. The Mart—like the other decaying buildings along Fruitvale, like Ruby and Diane—was young once. It had more memories than aspirations.

Tino opened the covers on the trash bins. The plastic bags were full of towels and McDonald's bags. He put new bags in the empty bins and tossed the full bags into the dumpster. The peace was broken by a burst of red and blue lights rushing toward him down Sixteenth Ave: no siren, only the whir of engines and rubber on an empty street. The police car slowed before the intersection and sped onto Fruitvale. Tino walked quickly out past the fuel stations, to the weathered sidewalk, and watched as the patrol turned into a lot up the road, into the Liberty, a mini-mart a few blocks west. He said a prayer and told God to have mercy. No one should die at a convenience store.

5:45 A.M.

The Mart and the town woke at the same moment. Tino, an hour earlier, dormant and drifting, now flurried between aisles and the counter. He finished his cleaning, devoured two sausage and cheese biscuits, and started a rack of hot dogs. He loaded cookie sheets full of breakfast burritos, sausage pizza rolls, and egg biscuits. He changed the filters and grounds on the coffee machines—two regulars and a decaf. He filled the garbage with discarded tin cans, wrappers, plastic casings, and expired food.

The Yakima sun began its return as the sky's sovereign, a role it took seriously in summer. Customers trickled, then flowed. The Mexicans came first, mostly construction workers or cherry pickers. They loaded up on chips and Pepsi. They filled plastic mugs with coffee and pop. Police officers and commuters followed. They finished one of the regular coffees and consumed the first two batches of breakfast taquitos. At 6:00, Tino opened the beer case. Professionals peppered in with the farmworkers—Brown Suit with his pack of Orbit gum and single serving chardonnay; Gray Beard with his self-refill, 32-ounce coffee; Orson Welles and his daily lust for Hawaiian Luau chips.

Once the flow started, it wouldn't stop. It would be like this until after 9:00, after Tino was back at his apartment debating between sleeping and another Xbox mission.

—"I have another batch in the oven. Five minutes."

—"I'll get that in a second."

—"Do you have anything smaller?"

—"Aisle Three, beside the Band-Aids."

6:50 A.M.

Tino looked up each time the doors opened but he no longer greeted. The Mart was too promiscuous. Graveyard was binge and purge, feast and famine. Tino longed for those early moments of nothingness, for the cool, concealing nighttime. Between running to the oven, mopping coffee spills, and restocking condiments, he glanced at the clock.

7:02 A.M.

Mary held the door for a construction worker in an orange shirt. She flirted with him, smiling and saying something about how hot it was supposed to get. Tino meant to ask how she ended up managing The Mart. Mary—petite, blond, Macy's-off-the-rack Mary. She walked to the rear of the store, taking the long path through Aisle Six before moving to the cooler and pulling a Monster energy drink. She stood in line behind Maple Bar. She straightened each display as she edged closer to Tino.

"Mornin'." She set the can on the counter and handed Tino a five-dollar bill. "Busy?"

Tino gave her change. "Last hour or so. Pretty normal night."

Mary took the Monster and the change and walked around the line into the back room. She set her purse on her desk. She checked her phone messages, looked at Diane's inventory sheet, and put an apron over her white blouse. When she came to store side of the counter, she carried a can of liquefied cheese, a fresh box of sausage taquitos, and a plastic money tray. She loaded the cheese and started the oven as Tino handled the surge of customers. "Diane left a message," she said.

"Yeah?" said Tino.

"She said you weren't taking the cleaning schedule seriously."

"Oh?" Tino pressed buttons on the cash register. It printed a stream of receipts. He opened the drawer and removed the money tray. Mary stepped toward it and inserted her tray. She entered a code as Tino untied his smock.

"Did you see the inventory sheet?" asked Mary. "According to Diane, we have forty-six cans of eggs."

"I think she meant Pepsi," said Tino.

"Will you do the coolers tonight?" asked Mary.

"Diane won't be happy."

Mary said she would explain things to Diane, but it did little to comfort Tino. This would only add to Diane's paranoia. Diane would think it was all part of Tino's ploy to take the swing shift, that he had forged errors onto the inventory sheet to become Mary's Number Two.

Tino gathered his keys from the backroom before buying a chili-cheese dog and a bottle of Cherry Coke. "See you tomorrow," he said.

Tino opened the right-side glass door and returned to his decaying Toyota. He set his food on the roof as he unlocked the doors. He didn't know why he bothered to lock them. He didn't have anything worth stealing. The car was cool for the moment. Tino closed the door, buckled, and took a bite of his hot dog. He rolled down his window and looked back at his store. "I'll see you tonight," he said. The Mart did not speak.

FIRST DAY
42ND AVE AND NOB HILL

She's my little girl and maybe I'm being selfish, but I don't want her to go. Once this happens, everything is different. In an hour, she'll have a new woman in her life telling her how to act and talk and where to sit. I know it's not the same thing—that a teacher isn't a mother—but Libby's the kind of girl who worships easily. She draws pictures of her Sunday school teacher and calls Ms. Kelly "the most beautiful woman in the world." She asks if she can live with the pastor's wife, and—I know this is wrong—it always hurts. If I didn't know better, I'd think she was testing weapons for her teen years. It comes honestly, and it's not that I wouldn't deserve it. By the time I was twelve, I knew all my mom's soft spots. I could drop her with a slow exhale.

I know it's not rational. Todd tells me not to get upset and that Libby doesn't mean anything by it. He reminds me how Libby said I could be a queen, how she curled up with me on the couch to watch TV, how she stroked my head and said, "Mommy, I want hair like yours." And it all helps, but it doesn't fix it. Until now, I've been her life, and that sounds terrible, I know—but I was her world, her only complete picture of womanhood, the only one she could love and look to. In an hour, she'll start comparing me—whether she means to or not. I know how it sounds, like I'm insecure and terrible, like I'm accusing my five-year-old of adultery.

Libby woke like it was Christmas morning, early and eager. She bounced into the bedroom and hovered over us. She whispered, "Is it time?"

Todd helped her with cereal while I cleaned up in the bathroom. They talked in the kitchen, and Libby asked if she was pretty enough. She asked if she could pick out her own clothes and Todd told her, "You and Mommy already decided what to wear last night. That dress is for church." Libby said she wanted to be beautiful for her new teacher and how the other girls would wear dresses. She said something about jeans being for boys and that she didn't want to dress like a boy or no one would talk to her. And all I could think was how does she know this stuff? Where do those ideas come from? Maybe it's genetic. God help her.

Todd came in to say he was leaving for work and that Libby had a bowl of cereal and half an apple. She was on the couch watching TV and sorting through her backpack. She was wearing the green taffeta dress we bought her for Easter.

"It's too short now," I said.

"She has her pink tights on underneath. It's not like she's a Bratz doll," said Todd.

I cried.

I'm a horrible person, I know. And there's no reason to cry because my little girl wants to wear a dress. In four years, she'll refuse to wear one, like I did. It will fulfill Mom's prophecy: "One day you'll have your own daughter. One day you'll understand."

But we had decided the night before—together, mother and daughter—that she would wear the new jeans from ShopKo and the yellow T-shirt from Mom, the one with the pink flower. She would wear her pink sneakers and the matching pink cardigan. It's September, and it's cool in the mornings, but by 3:00 it will be 90 degrees and she'll need something lighter, something she can play in.

Todd held my shoulder and told me that it's nothing. He kissed Libby on his way out and left us two girls in the house.

I pulled on jeans, the bra from the floor, a mostly clean T-shirt, and an old college sweatshirt. Libby was on the floor in her dress, sitting cross-legged and talking to her school supplies. She was that little cartoon bilingual girl on the TV, and she named each of her new tools in two languages. We had spent the night before reviewing the supply list, hoping everything was right. The school sent us a list in Spanish, but most of the things were easy to figure out: "crayones" and "Kleenex." I remembered, from high school, that "lápices" were pencils. I searched online for "mochila," "tijeras," and "pegamento."

Libby looked up. I could see it already. She was ashamed of me—how I hadn't even bothered to dress for her first day, how I didn't understand that I needed a gown, that kindergarten was the princess ball. "Is that what you're wearing?" she said. It begins that way.

She asked when we would leave. She asked me to say her teacher's name again and asked—again—if she would know anyone at school from church.

"Libby," I said, "you're so beautiful." She smiled at me, like she needed me to say it.

—"We're leaving in twenty minutes."

—"Your teacher is Ms. Thompson."

—"I don't think anyone from church will be there, but

you'll make new friends right away. Now put everything back into your backpack, so we're ready."

I asked if she wouldn't be more comfortable in the outfit we had picked out.

"It's not pretty enough," she said.

I made her lunch: a peanut butter sandwich, half a Fuji apple, fish crackers, and a baggie of M&Ms. I put a juice pouch inside. A napkin. Then clicked the lunch box shut. I had done this for Todd when we first married.

Libby came into the kitchen, stared up at me in those perfect oak-brown eyes, and said, "I'm ready Mom." She did not speak for me.

Todd and Libby had planned the path to school, walking along the broken sidewalk, shuffling around glass shards, litter, and goatheads, puncturevines—those terrible little weeds that poke through Libby's bike tires. "Are you sure you don't want to take the car?" I said.

"Mom, we timed it. Daddy said it is shorter to walk."

The sun was already bold, but it hadn't burned the cool away yet. Dew still sat on the grass. I held Libby's lunch box in my left hand and her hand in my right, guarding her from the stream of cars flying down Nob Hill. It was so dangerous: leaving our house at the moment everyone else did.

Libby rehearsed her alphabet. She counted to 47 before I asked her about what she wanted to do for dinner that night: "It's your first day," I said. "We'll have to celebrate." She would say McDonald's.

Libby's black dress shoes were getting dirty. When she walked through the grass, they become damp, and then the sidewalk dirt clung to them. My mother would have never been this forgiving. She would have made me stop and clean them.

The weeds grew between the sidewalk and the fence. They crept through every crack in pavement, forcing cracks where the pavement didn't want to yield. That's Yakima. It's the pavement and the weeds, fighting each other. And now I was offering Libby to that city, to be part of that system, and, oh God, what does that say about me? Maybe we should have taken her to the Christian school with her friends. We could have found the extra money. Scholarships were available.

We walked past the monstrous dental clinic, the one made to look like an amusement park. Libby always asked to play there, but not today. It used to be a drive-in movie theater, and when I went to community college, my friends and I would pile into a car, turn on the radio, and watch movies outside at night. Libby would probably never see a drive-in.

It took us eleven minutes to reach Whitney Elementary, two minutes longer than Libby and Todd had timed it. Libby let go of my hand to run across the grass toward her classroom. I called her back. Libby pleaded to show me around. She offered me the tour she and Todd received for orientation. She described the bulletin board outside her classroom, the pink butcher paper with construction-paper apples labeled with each student's name. Hers had a little green worm, she said, "with a smiley face." She faced me, walking backwards, chattering about field trips and recess and math.

The building behind her was a vast single-level school assembled, like Legos, in tight-fitted, light-colored brick. There were countless windows bordered by white pains and shutters, all designed to make a government building look like a comforting rambler. It was topped by a gable roof, painted a fashionable and friendly teal, and covered with composite shingles. To the unsuspecting, it may have looked like a home.

Large open fields and five-foot chain link fences surrounded the main building. On our side there was a smaller section, a private playground to protect the kindergartners from the older children. There was a slide, a little play dome, and a basket for balls. The grass was freshly mowed, kept in perfect order like a park or a cemetery.

Three blond girls raced around a dwarf Alder tree and, for a moment, I understood why Libby wanted to be here, to have her own place and her own world. She needed to be among other four-footers, with girls who wanted to dress up and boys who needed a place to stick their tongues out. Libby needed a field—her own fenced plot of land—to run in and play tag with people who weren't her mother.

The part of me that is a good mother released her and followed. I let her lead and show me the apple board and her classroom. I let her tell me how she would run through the field. She promised not to get her dress dirty. We walked between the white halls, surrounded by dozens of little boys with messy hair and runny noses and little girls who tricked their fathers into letting them wear dresses. They had formed a colony here and they welcomed one another as if they had a deeper blood connection than mothers and daughters would ever know. These were her people now.

Ms. Thompson wore a yellow long-sleeve turtleneck covered by a denim overall dress. She was an older woman, probably in her late forties, and she smiled to the children and told them to find their seats and to show their parents around the room. She shook my hand and said how happy she was to have Libby. She crouched down to her knees and faced my little girl, eye to eye, and shook her hand. She told her to find her desk and "show your Mom where you'll be sitting."

"We're so happy that you're sharing Libby with us," she said.

I didn't hate her.

Libby was right about walking. I wasn't ready to be in a car, taking a left turn into traffic. Libby looked so happy at her chair, so free, as if I had been her captor all these years. I wondered if she would think of me during the day or feel a tinge of guilt or beg Ms. Thompson to call me and say she missed me. I reached into my jeans and retrieved the cell phone, just to be sure it was on. The school had my number. Libby could call at any time.

I touched the phone to make sure it was working and thought of calling Todd to check the line. Just in case. But Todd would think I was crazy. He would ask what was going on and how the send-off went. He wouldn't know what to do when I cried, the second time before 9:00 a.m. I scanned through the directory, and found the only number that could comfort, or, at least, could understand. I pressed the green *send* button and held the phone to my ear, listening to the rings while walking around a crushed paper bag, half-praying that Mom wouldn't answer.

PERSONA, OR ALL SANCTUARIES SMELL LIKE STOCKHOLM
6TH AVE AND WALNUT

MONDAY

John stepped out of the shower and inhaled the sauna-like air—air humid and laced with deodorant and soap. Cleansing. He paused. Held. Released. He formed the exiting (expiring) air into his finest Max von Sydow accent: "My name ees Yo-han. My fay-vrit sit-ee ees Stohk-ome." *Again.*

Each syllable equal. Staccato. Hint of a roll to the 'r,' but not a Spanish roll. Breathe in. Gentle. Breathe out. Be natural. Be Swedish.

But a flat, accentless mother's voice called from beyond the door and reminded John that he was only John and that he was going to be late for school. John broke communion with his almost-Scandinavian self. Much more work remained to undo his sixteen years without an exotic heritage.

John toweled off, dressed, brushed his teeth. He left the bathroom, retrieved his coat and backpack, and tied a cyan-and-yellow scarf around his neck. It would be cold outside. Cold like Sweden, land of John's ancestors (*like Grandfather, like Ingmar Bergman.*)

November seeped through his coat, through his store-brand jeans, through his flag scarf. Longer nights and a cooler, clearer moon were overcoming the sun that bleached paint and burned grass in central Washington. The quieter season had come. White, frosted lawns. Fog breath. Holidays. Advent. *Is Advent Christmas or the coming of Christmas?*

John pulled a mess of wires from his pocket. White coated cables hung from his ears like a stethoscope. The walk brought tranquility. Eight blocks of controlled atmosphere, of music chosen for him (by him)—a soundtrack with John, the protagonist, worthy of his own theme. He programmed a Bach piece. It was an attempt to undo years of alternative rock and his sister's dance pop. He could almost recognize, sometimes even enjoy, the warmth of the Brandenburg Concerto's second Allegro. He scheduled *St. Matthew's Passion* for winter, the perfect score for the gap between Christmas (*Advent? Epiphany?*) and his first Lenten season.

John walked east down Spruce toward the Community of Christ Church: the last outpost of public underage smoking in Yakima. For some reason, the police and school did little to stop it. The Church was holy ground or sacred ground or some Switzerland. No adult set foot during a weekday, and no student loitered on Sabbaths. Perhaps the elders assumed the teens were coffee-drinking, cigarette-smoking refugees of an A.A. meeting.

"John," said Tina, the white girl with short black hair—the one who stood between Jorge and Aaron, just to the rear of Mike and Randall. She was the one in black leggings and black boots and a black sweater. She was the one with the black coat and black eyeliner. John watched her pull away from the stucco wall, a shadow escaping its master, as she drew on her cigarette.

John could not tell if the clouds around her were smoke or breath or if they were her own smoke or breath or that of the eight other smokers. He had a vision of these orphans at seventy, sagging and talking—through those strange robotic voice boxes—about sex and music and good ol' days with the other patients in the cancer ward. Mike would hit on the nurse, and Randall would show his faded, blurred tattoos, and Tina…. *What would become of Tina?*

John lifted his chin from his scarf and nodded at Tina. It was a faint nod, but Tina would see it. He looked toward the mascara where Tina's eyes should be. He buried his hands deeper into his coat pockets.

"John." *It's Randall calling. Only Randall.* John bobbed his head as if the music were too loud.

"Hey, Yo-han," said Jorge. *Why does he say it that way? He used to go by George, but no one laughs at* Hor-hey.

"Yo-han."

John glanced—an acknowledgment, a wink—toward Jorge, the tall Mexican with a shaved head and an unconvincing goatee. Jorge wore his usual matching set of denim jeans and jacket.

John looked both ways before crossing the street. He dropped the headphone from his left ear. He stepped toward the church, toward the nicotine fog.

"Hey, Jorge," said John. And to Jorge's right. "Tina."

"What'cha listening to?" said Aaron. Besides Jorge, he was the only non-white in the group, Indian. *Native American, not India Indian. Yakama, not Yakima.*

"Swans," said John, because Aaron thought Swans was the greatest band in existence. "Some War on Drugs and—." He looked at Tina for approval. *What was her band again? Wenatchee, Wednesday.* "Waxahatchee."

"We might skip first period," said Jorge. "Mike has his mom's car."

"I can't," said John. "I have Pre-calc. Mr. Thompson knows

my mom, so she might find out."

"Maybe tomorrow," said Jorge.

"Do you wanna smoke?" said Aaron.

"No, thanks," said John. "I better go. I'm on third floor."

"Hey, Yo-han," said Jorge. "How's your sister? She doesn't walk by here anymore."

"Meg's fine. She comes early for zero-period—Advanced Poetry or something." John fidgeted and shivered. "I better go. Cold."

"Hey, Yo-han," said Jorge. "Cómo se dice, *Later* in Swedish?"

"Hej då."

"Okay, Yo-han. Hey du-ah," said Jorge.

John stepped away. He snuck his right hand from his coat pocket and attempted an underhand wave to Tina. She pulled the cigarette from her black lips, lifted her bloodless hand, and returned the signal.

John crossed Seventh Avenue—the moat surrounding the walls of A. C. Davis High School—the boundary that separated the castle from the modern world. He hid his headphones before one of the corrupt sheriffs could confiscate them.

At lunch, John found Tina and Jorge and a few of the other church smokers still on campus. They usually went to someone's house or to KFC or to one of the fifty mini-marts in town. But Jorge was sitting at one of the collapsible benches in the multi-purpose room. He ate from a pale-yellow plastic tray, his food separated into little compartments. Tina sat to his left, Mike and Aaron to his right.

John thought Tina seemed somehow both pleased and terrified to see him. So John sat with the smokers. He pulled a sandwich and a bag of Fritos from his bag, a lunch his Mom had thrown in while he was taming his cowlick and practicing dialect. Jorge helped himself to a Frito while Tina sat and chewed on an unnaturally jaundiced pile of potatoes and turkey gravy.

"I didn't think you guys would be here," said John.

"Tina didn't want to leave," said Jorge. "She said she wasn't feeling well."

"I hate eating here," said Mike. "It's creepy. The Nazis in the office probably have hidden cameras."

"Johan," said Jorge. "Has Tina always been so moody?"

Tina was unmoved. She stirred her potatoes with her fork. *Was she always? We were other people. She left first.*

"We don't really hang out much anymore," Tina said, saving John. "We used to go to the same church."

"Damn," said Aaron. "You go to church?"

"Used to."

"Maybe you should go back," said Jorge. "Confess your sins." Tina reached back, balled her fingers, and slammed Jorge's left arm. She picked up her tray, tossed it and the food into a black-bagged trash can, and walked out of the lunchroom. Jorge watched her go and massaged his arm and smiled.

"Man, Jorge," said Mike, "You're not getting any today."

TUESDAY

John detoured past the church. He had nothing to say this morning. He was too tired to fake a smile or interest or an excuse for not skipping class or hanging out at lunch. He walked east, down Tieton, and entered the campus from the park. John followed the cement walkway into the cement courtyard, past the cement benches, toward one of the cement stairways. He scaled each step, avoiding eye contact with packs of red-hooded boy-men (and blue-hooded boy-men).

He reached the third floor. The janitors had painted the lockers, again. They covered the markings in beige latex, a futility that would be undone before the day's final bell. By Wednesday, John's locker would have a new spray-painted *XIV* already scratched out with a key. By Thursday, there would be a fresh *XIII* or *CPV* or some other territorial pissing. It didn't really matter to John. The gangs rarely touched the white kids.

The hallway filled with other students murmuring about the new layer of paint or the cold or their neglected homework. Two sophomore girls stood back-to-back texting other people. They took shifts, keeping watch so that a teacher wouldn't surprise them and take their phones. A couple of juniors exchanged last minute gropings. Two freshmen talked about a new *Star Wars* rumor.

"Hey," said Tina, standing behind John. It was a whisper. John turned. Tina was pretty, or still held the form of prettiness. Dark prettiness.

"We're skipping first period. You should come," she said.

"I can't," he said.

"Is it because Jorge or Aaron?"

Yes and yes.

"They'll be good," she said. "You should come."

"I really have to go to class," he said. *I know I shouldn't, but I should.*

"Please, John."

"You have Jorge and Mike and Aaron," he held steady, like a real man.

"John."

"I can't," he said. *Ask one more time, please. Make me go.*

WEDNESDAY

John avoided the smoker's church again, though this time with a real reason. He had walked this other route every Wednesday and Friday since school started, since he had returned from the summer with his father, since he declared he was a Lutheran named Johan. *Did your father tell you to do this? He doesn't care about church. He's never cared.*

Bethlehem Lutheran was a red-brick building one block from the high school. John imagined these bricks were made from holy soil and purified by fire. There was no cloud of student smoke at Bethlehem. Perhaps it was too close to a main road for the smokers. Maybe it was because on Wednesday and Friday mornings the church opened the doors to students, offering juice and donuts and fruit and a chance to escape the cold. It was a shelter. John needed shelter.

"Good morning, Pastor Beck," said John.

"Hi, John. Do you want to help the Wilsons set out the food?"

"Sure."

John walked through the opening lobby. *It is the narthex or the nave?* He walked down a hallway, past classroom doors and the pastor's study, to the fellowship hall. Compared to the sanctuary, the hall looked unfinished. John thought it was the one place in the church that could have been built by Baptists. He wondered if all fellowship halls looked the same, if in every Christian church there is one designated coffee-scented room for collapsible brown tables, white walls, and old prints of robed/bearded Jesus as a shepherd.

John greeted Mr. Wilson. He had always meant to ask him what he did for a living—if he was retired, why he was here, why he was always happy. *Will I wear purple sweaters when I'm his age?*

Mr. Wilson set plastic forks on a table. He walked toward John with a full smile and an extended hand. John joined his hand: a quick, firm shake. "Laura's getting the last tray together. Could you help her finish cutting Danishes?"

John agreed and walked into the kitchen to see the tall, elegant woman, cutting a pastry into perfect quarters. Two confident cuts. A white collar topped her purple sweater. *Always a matching pair. Always here.*

Other students appeared. John recognized Alice Jensen. They were in band together as ninth graders. There were a few younger boys, lifelong Lutherans, homeschoolers who live nearby. *Is it Dan and Don or Dave and Doug?* "Hey guys," John said. Sometimes Gerry Thompson showed up, but not this morning. Then there was Robert Page, the one guy that no one ever doubted—the alpha male, the guy who captured all the good Teutonic spirit that birthed Lutheranism. He looked twenty-five, solid like a wrestler, and he wore jeans and a leather jacket and a Fugazi shirt. Robert had a short mohawk that would have been false on a lesser person. He was the smartest and politest of the Lutheran youth. He loved the Wilsons and the pastor, and he loved confession, and he closed his eyes when he took the bread and wine. He crossed himself afterward. Robert also loved denim and leather and old punk bands and would take communion in a Black Flag shirt. *If I could be someone else, I'd be Robert.*

The Wilsons and Pastor Beck ate and talked with the students and, for a moment, the ages and experiences and identities disappeared.

Some of the older members arrived. When the elders outnumbered the young, they left the fellowship hall and went into the sanctuary for communion. It was open to all who would come, though, except for Robert and Alice, none of the high schoolers took part. It was usually the Wilsons and Paul Thomas—a Korean War vet, always in an olive-green Army jacket—and a few businessmen and women on their ways to work.

John had not yet taken Lutheran communion. He was still in membership classes and making up for missing Confirmation. But he liked to watch this strange ritual. He liked believing that the bread and wine turned into the body and blood of Christ for the forgiveness of sins. *For all sins?*

He liked being in the sanctuary. The air was quiet. Aged. Somehow, it mingled with the wood pews and the altar and the ornaments and images—perhaps it was changed by the mist of sacramental wine and crumbs of blessed bread (*blood of Christ, body of Christ*). Had John felt surer about it, he might have said "holy" air. He thought of how Tina had described smoking to him and how she said that, at first, when you breathe in the smoke, it fills the lungs and the arms and the neck—it's like the body releases you for a moment of peace. *Maybe that's the nature of smoking: that it causes an evil like cancer because it promises what only sacramental air should offer.*

The final bell created chaos—as if the students were Eisenhower-era laborers freed from the production line. The dayshift gathered lunchboxes and scurried toward cars and buses. They flowed into the halls, the smell of new spray paint mixed with perfume and department store body spray and perspiration. Shouting, singing, whispering. A symphony of mundane noises. Slamming metal lockers, squeaking hallway exits, crumpled papers littering the floor. Then, like the calm after a car crash, stillness.

John stayed by his locker. He searched it. Perhaps Tina had dropped a note through the vents. He hadn't seen her since Tuesday morning. *Maybe she'll come back. She knows where my locker is.* He played movies in his head, the cheesy American kind: he watched the couple that was supposed to meet up and how there was a delay and the girl missed the boy by a half second—a turned corner—which led to ninety minutes of rejection and pain and misunderstanding. But John had no right to expect Tina. This was no movie and there was no misunderstanding. John had been very clear.

John closed his locker and descended the brick-and-concrete citadel. He walked slowly, scanning courtyard and walkways. He crossed Seventh in search of his favorite of the Church Nine. Jorge was there. Mike and Aaron, Leonard and Cindy. There was Steve and another girl John didn't recognize.

"Yo-han. Qué pasa?" said Jorge.

"Hey," said John. "Where's Travis and Tina? I haven't seen Tina since this morning."

"Travis is home watching his little sister," said Aaron.

"Tina," said Jorge. "She said she wasn't feeling good. Smoke?"

John waived the cigarette away.

"How come you never stay?" said Jorge.

"I just always have to be somewhere, I guess."

"Do you have to be somewhere right now?" said Jorge.

John flirted with telling the truth, with saying that his Mom wouldn't be home until after five and that Meg was at volleyball and that no one in the world knew or cared what he did weekday afternoons. *It sounds like an invitation.*

"My mom's sorta a neat freak. I gotta clean the bathroom, like scrub the toilet and stuff. I'm probably already late." He scrambled, adding more to his story. "And I have a Pre-Calc test tomorrow that I have to study for, so I better get going. Is it three already?" John made a quick glance to the wrist where a watch could be. "Maybe tomorrow."

THURSDAY

John tortured his reflection. He stared at his eyes that should be blue and his hair that should be blonde. He cursed the face cursing at him. He was mad at Johan, at John. *Where is she? Why didn't she just ask one more time?*

John criticized the clothes—the bland wardrobe accented by a dull head filled with a mediocre mind. *Gentle. Gentle. Breathe.*

John walked to the smoker's church. He even crossed on the north sidewalk, right in front of the group. The cloud was smaller. He counted. Eight. No Tina. *Eight. There was room for one more if Tina didn't show. But why join? Why breathe in death and meaninglessness if there's no Tina?*

"Hey, Johnny," said Jorge, touching John's neck. John had forgotten his scarf. Jorge corrected himself. "Yo-han." Jorge said he had seen Meg and asked if she was a senior.

"Yeah," said John. "She's picking out colleges." The faint sound of a violin floated from John's headphones as they hung down his shoulders. He tried to identify the music, tried to find some comfort in the scraps of treble that linked him to a home he had never seen in color.

"Can I ask you a question," said Jorge. John nodded. *Isn't that a question?* "What do you think about Meg and me? I never see her with a guy, so I figure she isn't seeing anyone."

"I don't know," said John. "She seems pretty serious about not dating, since she broke up with Glen."

"Good to know."

"Hey, Aaron," said Mike. "Georgey-boy is trying to bone Johnny's sister." Aaron laughed as Jorge shot a keep-it-cool/not-in-front-of-the-brother glance. *Dear God. Please don't make me related to Jorge.*

"What about Tina?" said John.

"She's a little weird."

"You still together?"

"I don't know. Haven't seen her since Tuesday. I think she's still sick or something."

"I got class," said John.

"Always to class, Yo-han. It's not the real world. You know that, right?" *Real world. What does that even mean?* "We need to hang out," said Jorge.

"Yeah, soon."

"Hey, John," Jorge said. "Say Hi to Meg."

John stood on the third-floor balcony. He watched over the courtyard, where there was a statue of William O. Douglas—Justice Douglas—a Yakima native, a Davis graduate who served on the Supreme Court for thirty years. *Was this even the same school then?* There were others. There was a writer called Raymond Carver, and there was a movie made from some of his stories. He went to Davis and he became something, someone. He never came back. There was Joe Hipp, the big Indian guy—a Blackfoot, not even a Yakama. He was a boxer, a real boxer. Sometimes, Joe stopped by the school so people could ask him about beating "Bigfoot" Martin. Only Joe Hipp came back, but he didn't get a statue.

John wasn't high enough to say they all looked like ants. They still looked like students, like people. Some he even recognized. There was Peter Thompson, in his Navy pea-coat. There was Jaime Salvado, shivering in his hooded sweatshirt, more afraid to cover the red than to freeze to death. They were best friends in fourth grade. There was Gale Smith, an androgynous junior who only hung out with other androgynous girls until softball season. She and Meg used to be friends.

Most were anonymous. The four black girls followed by guys in orange lettermen jackets. There were the musicians, emerging from zero-period band. There were a few Yakamas, aliens in a land that once belonged to them. The country boys—the cowboys. And then there were administrators and teachers and security patrols trying to appear friendly, but always watching, always on guard against a lawsuit.

But no Tina.

FRIDAY

Bethlehem Lutheran was still foreign to John, especially since for ten years—since the divorce—his family went to the Baptist church. To John, Christianity spread through pop songs and grape juice and announcements, through multimedia lectures about making Jesus the Lord of his life. He was used to the youth group and playing games and telling stories and talking about making, "God-honoring decisions." *Sex. Always sex. Not even Mike and Aaron talked about sex as much as youth group.*

John didn't want to talk. He wished it was Wednesday. He wished he was ready to take communion. There was something wrong in him, almost like a sin worth forgiving.

He snatched a blueberry bagel and a paper cup of orange juice. He greeted Pastor Beck and the Wilsons and a couple of the old ladies he recognized from Sunday mornings. He ate and exited, past Robert and his mohawk, into the hallway. He looked at the classroom doors and how the church seemed dormant. He wandered into the narthex and stared at the doors: doors that opened, right, to Tieton / doors that opened, left, to the sanctuary.

The sanctuary was dark, lit only by a bulb near the altar and the emerging sun charging the stained glass—Jesus in a boat. The tobacco-colored pews, slowly warming, exchanged small creaks like waking trees. The altar was empty.

In the third row was the silhouette of head and shoulders, a pilgrim or vagrant who had claimed solitude before John could. The head—the dark, short-haired head—shifted briefly and looked back. The shape turned forward again, facing the altar. A bodiless voice floated in the air.

"John."

"Tina?"

John moved toward her, stepping in and out of the light, watching the great room for apparitions of saints. He sat on the edge of the pew, only a breath from Tina, or someone that looked like Tina. She was stripped of her raccoon mask. Her eyes were hazel. *Yes, that was the color.* The mascara and lipstick were absent, and Tina's face was pink and plain. The skin had contours and acne—flaws usually concealed by pancake powder.

This version of Tina was unfinished. Undecorated. There was something privileged or improper about looking at her. John wasn't supposed to see her this way, unadorned, unmarked, unveiled for the presence of God. He had a sense of how a woman's exposed calf muscle awakened Puritan passion. He understood a Muslim man's desire when removing his wife's covering, discovering her hidden, flowing hair. Tina's innocence, her nakedness, made John hazy with wonder and shame.

He sat beside her, holding his hands together, restraining them from reaching for her cheeks or lips. He calmed his heart. *Gentle. Gentle. Breathe.*

They sat in silence, with eyes parallel, staring to the altar. They needed a word—permission to split the air with more than recognition. And John, in a moment he couldn't understand, unclasped his hands and slid his left toward her right and his fingers covered her fingers and the two frozen adolescent fists formed a warm nest where life could be nurtured. Neither flinched.

Tina inhaled. She drew her breath, a full breath. She released, and she said—or maybe it was the building that said—"I'm pregnant."

John heard but didn't speak. He kept his hand holding hers and let the words ring and he thought about what they meant and, in a moment of grace, he didn't think to ask who the father was or whether she told her parents or what she was going to do. He only sat.

John felt Tina turn. Maybe he felt the air move. He shifted toward her, gazing at her chin. His eyes ascended her face, chin to lip, lip to lip, lip to nose and then to the eyes—foreign yet familiar hazel eyes.

"Do you remember all those videos they used to show, back in youth group?" she said. "They used to tell us our bodies were temples and that the world would try to destroy the temples. They used to say how God wanted us to be pure."

John nodded.

"Do you think God is angry at me?"

It was a simple question, but John couldn't form a yes or no. He didn't have a right to answer. *How would I know? If he's mad at you, he must hate me.*

"I'm sorry I didn't go with you Tuesday," John said.

Tina lowered her head. She tightened her grip on John's hand.

"It's okay," she said.

"Is that when you found out?"

"That's when I knew."

"Jorge said you were sick."

"That's how Jorge would describe it."

John faced the empty altar. On Wednesday and Sunday Christ would come there. He would offer his flesh. His forgiveness. *Nothing on Friday.*

"There's a movie I saw this summer—when I stayed with my dad," said John. He paused, waiting for Tina to tell him to stop or go on. She said nothing. John, having no better idea, continued.

"It's about this pastor and he doesn't believe in God, and he asks, 'Why have you forsaken me,' just like Jesus did. And God doesn't say anything. So the pastor thinks that means God's not real. So he tells this fisherman maybe nothing matters. The pastor actually says that, and the fisherman loses all hope. So, he shoots himself by the river—'cause he's scared of nuclear war or something. And if God doesn't care, why should he?"

John waited. Tina breathed—consent to continue.

"It turns out that the pastor's wife had died, and he couldn't see God after that. But he keeps doing his job. He gets up every Sunday. He does the Lord's Supper and he tells people the wine they drink is the blood of Jesus and that their sins are forgiven. Some people believe it, and some don't. But he still gives it out, because, even if he doesn't believe it, that's what he's supposed to do."

John swallowed. He hadn't said this many words to another person in months.

"At the end, there's this hunchback guy, and he's in a lot of pain and he tells the pastor that he doesn't think the torture and crucifixion were the worst parts of Jesus' death. He said he thought it was feeling forsaken by God and his friends and how that suffering must be the greatest suffering a person can experience."

Tina squeezed John's hand. "Do you believe that? About suffering?" she said.

"Maybe." *Yes, I do believe that.* "Maybe it's true. Or maybe it's just the way they think in old Swedish films. I can't explain why, but I understood it, the way that I can't explain why I'm here, in this church, but I understand it."

"You understand Swedish films?"

"Not Swedish, like the language, but how Swedish movies feel," John said. "Something about them. My Dad has dozens of those movies. I watched them all summer. He was off at work, and I was home alone because Meg didn't come and I can't drive. So I just watched those movies. There was this one about a girl who goes crazy and thinks God is a spider. And there's another one about a knight playing chess with death. I tried to learn chess, but I suck at it."

"Is that the deal with *Johan?*" said Tina.

"Dad told me about how my grandfather came from Sweden. Mostly I just think of those movies, and they make me feel more alone but more not alone."

"So you're acting Swedish."

"I am Swedish. At least more than anything else. A little Irish, a little French. A bunch of other stuff. But almost half Swedish."

"A mongrel, like the rest of us."

Like the rest of us. No, I come from somewhere.

"Maybe you should just join the film club," said Tina.

"Maybe."

"And this church?"

"Grandpa was Lutheran. He said no self-respecting Swede would be anything else. But Dad doesn't even go to church."

"And you?"

"But I like it here. It makes sense to me, like those movies."

"And what about 'Johan'?"

Tina was prettier than John remembered. He pictured himself kissing her cheek but did not move. Perhaps if he were Italian, if he were Giovanni, he would have seized her and caressed her and kissed her until she was enraptured, and the Church would glow with candles and summer warmth and a Mediterranean breeze. But he held the moment, held her hand,

and tried to memorize the image of her naked face.

"I haven't been in a church for a long time," said Tina. "Maybe the reason I feel dirty now is because of the way I was clean then."

"You should come here. Like on Sundays," said John.

"I don't think it's for me anymore. But I think it fits you." Tina reached her left hand into her pocket and pulled out her phone. "Four minutes 'til class."

John breathed in Tina and the wood and the stillness. *Was Jorge right about something? Maybe school doesn't matter.*

"Three minutes," she said.

"Maybe we should stay here," he said.

Tina clenched John's hand, and it warmed. "I think I love Jorge," she said.

John's grip softened, but he tried to sound strong, not envious—concerned, not petty: "Jorge doesn't even know you."

"No one does, John."

It was a slap. But John took it without blinking, without withdrawing. He considered it. Maybe Tina was right. Maybe he didn't know her. Maybe he didn't know anyone. But he would know after the pastor gave him the sacrament, after his mother accepted him, after his father returned home, after Tina left Jorge. He was close to being himself. For now, in this moment, he was almost John. *This is the John I want to be. "I think this is me, right here,"* he almost said. But he couldn't speak. So he held to Tina while she could be held—together and alone—and dwelled in a moment without high school or Jorge or divorce. No need or urgency. Only sanctuary. No shame, only sacrament. No persona. Only Tina and John amid air fragranced with divinity.

HERO
3RD ST AND YAKIMA

We stood at attention when the car drew close, and one of the nieces even saluted. I wondered who taught her that—if it was Maria. Someone said, "This is what you do at a Veterans Day parade, *mija*. Salute now. Your uncle is passing by." Like he was Atticus Finch.

Salute Pedro Gutierrez. Pedro, the gangbanger whose dying was the only noble thing he ever did. Pedro, who joined the Army to hide. Another day on the streets and the cousins of someone he jumped would have stabbed him. Or worse: there would be a drive-by that killed someone who mattered, someone like Maria and her family. My family. *Mi familia.*

If Pedro had died here, stabbed or shot or beaten, the people that stood on curbs, the ones who saluted his poster-size picture—riding in the back of a 1950-something Chevy like a Cuban dictator—those people would have said it was justice: one less punk. The karma of gang life. Let them kill each other. But Pedro died in Afghanistan, in the last gasps of America's longest war, and we saluted him as some lost American innocent in a shrapnel-shredded uniform. He was a hero. He was Maria's hero.

Maria waved at the car, and she walked out to it and touched its waxed white door. One of the men inside, a Vietnam vet with a black baseball hat, gave her a little flag on a kabob skewer. Maria brought it back to the curb, and she walked to

Javier, her father, and presented it to him. Javier held Maria like a son.

THE LAST TIME I WENT TO CHURCH WITH MY WIFE'S SISTER
4TH ST AND LINCOLN

Maria said the two of us should go without her. "You two always had a special bond," she said.

St. Joseph's was growing familiar, almost needed—like wine or a tomato soup, those things you avoid as a kid but crave as an adult. You develop an appetite. You don't want them daily, but sometimes you *need* a glass of merlot or a well-seasoned bisque, and nothing else in the world—not the things that were once the definition of flavor, not Pizza Hut or Twizzlers or Dr. Pepper—is filling.

Cristina loosened, finger-by-finger, her gloves then removed them in two quick moves and tucked them into her coat pocket. She dipped her finger into one of the metal bowls attached to the inside wall (there's probably a word for those bowls). She glazed the holy water across her forehead: up-down, left-right cross. I did the same. Then Cristina dipped again.

"Once is enough," I said.

"You can't overdose," she said.

When Cristina walked into the church, there was this small possibility, this reasonable view, that she resembled every other woman in the building. In the muted light of the sanctuary, a distant viewer could confuse her Italian coat with a common Old Navy coat. But with the coat off, Cristina's difference was obvious. The perfection of her black sweater. Her leopard-print skirt holding mid-thigh against black nylons. The sweater was grace—an homage to the spirit of Audrey Hepburn. The skirt was the alchemy of a great mixed drink: disparate and impossible elements matched to produce something transcendent.

Cristina knelt and crossed herself before entering the pew. The young Catholics stopped doing this, especially in the English Mass. But everyone over forty and everyone in the Spanish Mass did it. I knelt and crossed and sat beside Cristina. I left a space between, enough room for a missal. I took off my coat and set it to my left. Cristina laid hers to her right.

Cristina sat straight and watched the altar. Her black button-up sweater molded around her torso. It followed her shape. Delicate and fitted, with long, woven sleeves and black buttons up the front. The top two were undone, and Cristina's collar hung open, exposing the flesh between the hollow of her neck and the sleek, lifted slope of her breasts.

I settled back. Cristina leaned onto the pew in front of us. The fringe of her sweater rose. The space between sweater and waistband disclosed her skin, smooth and the color of an over-creamed coffee.

Cristina straightened, and the aperature closed like and eyelid.

She was my opposite. I wore Dockers I bought without trying on. A never-iron dress shirt, the kind with button collars. The outfit, if I should even use the term, was a chance assembly of modular clothes held together by a reversible brown/black belt with a stainless-steel buckle. I had bought everything with a store credit card to save fifteen percent. Maria gave me the shoes, a pair of Rockports, three Christmases ago. They were worth more than everything else—underwear and socks included.

The bulletin noted upcoming events, prayers, youth activities, and retreats. It listed the scripture readings, the Wednesday-night Advent service. We were still in Pentecost.

Cristina eased back into the pew. She shuffled her coat and pulled her phone from it. It had a pink case, and Cristina waved her finger across the phone's front. She held down a button at the top, and the phone went dark, then was returned to the coat pocket.

"You come here often?" I said.

Cristina smiled, but only with her lips—the eyes never changed. She opened her bulletin. She pulled up the missal and looked through the liturgy. The missal guided us, telling us what to say and when to say it. It told us when to be contrite and kneel or to be worshipful and stand or attentive and sit. You can, it said, sit instead of kneeling. Most people in the English Mass, when given the choice, sat. The missal told us what words we believed. We could say them if we agreed. We could say them if we did not.

The organist played the processional, and Cristina focused on the altar, unwavering. She was hungry. She was waiting for the body and blood, like she hadn't eaten in a week. I didn't think we were supposed to take it without Confession.

The Sharing of the Peace.

"Peace be with your spirit," I said.

We hugged, no coats separating her sweater and my shirt.

Cristina said, "Peace be with you." She still used the old words. The Pope changed the words five or six years ago, but Cristina would not change with them. She said the Church should not change its words. It should be the one place that does not adjust, the one place that remains what it was when you last went, that is the same for every generation—or how could you share a belief if the words changed. The words were like mountains. How can you know you're home if the mountains have moved.

I had no allegiance to words. When the priest wished the Lord be with us, I and the other parishioners said, "And with your spirit." Cristina said, "And also with you." She would not say, "Lord God of Hosts" because the old words—the words of belief—were "Lord of power and might."

At Eucharist, Cristina ushered me ahead of her. I took the wafer. It was a thin, perfect circle, and I couldn't imagine the first disciples eating it. But it was the words that were important. *This is the body and blood of Christ given for the forgiveness of sins.* I took the wine. I sipped and walked away. The priest wiped the chalice and handed it to Cristina. She reached up with two hands, afraid, maybe, that it would be taken from her before it hit her lips. She crossed herself.

I turned to see whether Cristina was following. She seemed to be studying the carpet. A middle-aged couple passed her.

At our pew, back at the coats, I stood. Cristina kneeled and crossed herself again when entering. She brushed past without looking up. She pulled out the kneeler and lifted her skirt and set her knees on the cushion. She leaned over the pew and stared at the altar we had just left.

I tried to see what Cristina saw. The parishioners received the sacrament then filed off. They were all taking the same wafers, the "bread," and believed—most of them, probably—that it was, somehow, the body of a man. Sometimes I believed it.

They were drinking from a shared cup. What tasted like boxed red wine was the blood of this same man. It was something mysterious and real. Sometimes I believed this, too.

Cristina slid back into the pew, her hips crossing the boundary left for the missal and sliding into mine. They were firm—firmer than her sisters'. She tilted her head and whispered, the warmth of her breath trailing from my ear down my neck, "It's amazing to think of all that can be forgiven."

"Yes," I said. "Maybe everything can be forgiven."

HOW HILLS LOOK FROM THE AIR
24TH AVE AND WASHINGTON

Winston always means well. That's why he's a good doctor and, for the most part, a good husband. But it's also why he's gullible, and this wouldn't be the first time he volunteered us for a mistake. So, I insisted on coming along. It's not that I don't trust him. I just didn't want to end up in some godforsaken village because my husband means well.

I'm not a complainer, but there are two things I won't let pass: lying and stupidity. That's how I've lived my life and that's why Winston is the man he is today. I remember the first time I saw him, head buried in a physiology book on the steps of O'Connell. We were at Boston College as Dukakis was ahead in the polls and we really thought we could save this country from the Bushes and Reagans, the lying and the stupid. I walked up to Winston, the thin but beautiful British-looking boy, clueless about the world around him. "Remember to register." I handed him a flyer. He pulled off his glasses, stared at me, and then glanced at the sheet.

"I don't really get into politics," he said.

Don't ask me how I knew, but I knew—even then: Winston Townsend was worth saving. I sat with him and explained how Reagan had waged secret wars, exploited the poor, and turned the environment into his own private garbage dump. "Bush will do the same if we don't stop him," I said.

We talked about what we wanted in our lives. I told him that

I was doing it—being in politics and public service was how I would make a difference. He said he wanted to be a pediatrician and go to South America to help the disadvantaged. We went out for coffee. We watched a few movies. Within a week, Governor Dukakis had another volunteer, and I had Winston (happy to break off with that beast, Sam Manchester). Winston would become more than a suffering missionary doctor.

Even now, I have to keep Winston's best interests at heart. When it came to Yakima, I wouldn't say Winston was stupid, but I was sure that Mitch, the too-accommodating career advisor was a liar. Mitch had found his way into Winston's sympathies, exploiting that college boy who fantasized about living in huts and casting broken arms.

The way Winston talked, Yakima was Shangri-La. But that's Winston: too trusting. He parrots everything people say, especially headhunters like Mitch. It's a miracle he's never joined a cult or signed us up for Amway. Mitch said, "Yakima is a place that will give you the chance to make a difference." So, Winston—a brilliant doctor, yes, but not especially shrewd with men like Mitch—said, "It's a place that will give me the chance to make a difference."

"Winston," I said, "What do you know about Yakima?"

"Mitch said it's the heart of Washington State. He said that it's just south of an 'Old West' college town and close to Seattle."

"How close?" I asked.

"Not sure," said Winston," but it must be pretty close because Mitch talked about how Seattle's better than Newark or Boston."

"Damn, Winston. Dorchester's better than Newark."

I asked about the weather, the population, and the

demographics—not that I have anything against minorities; my best friend in college was an eighth Cuban. Winston's every answer started with, "Mitch said," or "Mitch didn't say," or "I forgot to ask Mitch." So forgive me for being suspicious. Forgive me for thinking maybe Mitch wasn't trustworthy or Yakima wasn't the world's best-kept secret or that maybe Winston shouldn't be left alone for a weekend with Mitch in Yakima.

◆

"Boeing's from Seattle," said Winston.

I said that he probably didn't want me to associate the northwest with the miserable little 737 Mitch put us on. "It's a one-stop flight from Boston to Yakima," he said. "That's pretty impressive."

"I can get a nonstop to Detroit in a real airplane," I said. "I suppose that means we should move to Detroit."

Winston flipped through papers while I tried to rest. Still, he poked me whenever he came across some meaningless little statistic or glowing piece of propaganda about paradise in the frontier. "Did you know that there are three hundred days of sunshine per year?"

"What happens for the other sixty-five days?"

"There are over sixty wineries in the area," he said.

"Good. Doctors can get drunk locally."

"Yakima has 'an abundance of outdoor recreation, including fly-fishing, and is only miles away from great skiing, camping, and hiking,'" he said.

"Winston. The last time we went skiing, you sprained your ankle and got a fever," I said. "You've never gone fishing. You've never slept outside in your life, and your definition of 'rural' is Gloucester. What makes you think you'll go hiking?"

"Maybe I would like to try fishing," he said.

"Wake me when we get there."

✦

In general, I'm honest—maybe too honest. But I'm fair. So if anyone thinks I'm simply down on everything, let me be the first to say that I liked the airport, even if—compared to Logan—it's just a field and a barn. Mitch, on the other hand, was—and I'm being charitable—disappointing. I could stand a charlatan, a glossy pitchman with a steel heart and a bottomless expense account, but Mitch was nothing of the sort. He was a man that, at probably the same age as Winston, had never made a meaningful, disciplined decision in his life. He was what Winston could have been: a leaf floating where the stream took him, happy to embrace every current as the will of some providential hand. No one gets that fat without drifting and compromising.

Mitch stood outside the gate with a sign made of white copier paper with TOWNSEND written in blue marker—as if Winston were a co-ed on Spring Break, not one of the premier cardiologists in New England. Mitch was dressed in the most obvious of suits, a black two-piece that was clearly off-the-rack, bought because it fit arm length, not girth. There was no way that poor slab of polyester would button, and so it hung open, leaving the white, crinkled dress shirt to cover the vast sweep of Mitch's gut.

Winston waved to Mitch, and the bulging man smiled like a

strip-mall Santa as he waddled to us. He shook Winston's hand, said the general niceties about how it was wonderful to finally meet and, of course, asked about our flight. Mitch was like a disc jockey with a booming voice, a resounding warmth and authority that worked well on phone calls, the kind of man's voice that men respond to. But, like all radio personalities, the voice and body did not match.

"It's so nice to finally meet you," he said as he surrounded my hand in his monstrous fists. I swear there was barbeque sauce under his fingernails.

His grip was warm and full and he looked me in the eyes. But he was too assuming. Winston thought him friendly, but it's Mitch's job to be likeable. Winston couldn't see that Mitch was a used car salesman who wheeled-and-dealed professionals like Buicks.

"You'll have to forgive the weather," he said. "It's rained for three straight days. This almost never happens."

"What happened to the three hundred days of sunshine?" I said.

"I guess we'll have 297 this year," he said. Smug.

Mitch helped carry our luggage, which suited him. He walked us to a Lexus, and if I hadn't checked the plates, I would have thought it rented. Inside, the car had that faint pungent smell of cigarettes buried beneath pine and vanilla air fresheners. Mitch put our bags in the trunk as I took my spot in the back. From the rear, I could watch and listen as Mitch tried his pitches on Winston. When the car started, the radio was turned to some local talk program. The commentator said something like, "shot because he was wearing a red shirt." Mitch switched the channel. "Aerosmith," he said, finding a classic hits station. "Bad boys of Boston, right?"

"I scanned the Yakima paper online before we left," I said. "There was a lot about shootings."

"It's not like LA or anything," said Mitch. "They're getting it under control. Yakima's even been chosen as an 'All-American City' for creative solutions to crime." Mitch adjusted the rear view mirror, but not before I gave him a glance that let him know I wasn't an idiot. The essential element in "creative solutions to crime" is crime.

"One article said Yakima has the highest percentage of chlamydia and gonorrhea in the State," I said.

"I read that Disneyland has graffiti," said Mitch.

Winston, that well-meaning diplomat, broke in. "Now, Mitch, you said that Yakima has excellent restaurants. Jenny, you're going to love the Mexican food, and there's even a place in town with sushi." *Fine*, I thought. I'll give the place a chance.

Sometimes its important to remember that proximity does not mean similarity. Yakima is near Seattle, but that doesn't make it *like* Seattle. There aren't any real trees, just bushes, tumbleweeds, and a few pines. On the plane, in that in-between sleep one gets on planes, I transferred what I read about Seattle to Yakima, like they were both in Washington, so they shared family traits: the ocean smell, mountain peaks, and fresh food. I thought that if Yakima were a few miles away, it must have wild blackberries, cool summer breezes, and postcard images—a poor, but familiar, cousin of Seattle with clearer skies. But that's all wrong. There's no family resemblance. If anything, Yakima is Tucson's illegitimate daughter.

Mitch talked incessantly about the weather and the rain. He

apologized, but said that the farmers would want it and that the water made the hills "glow emerald like the great Scottish highlands." *Really.* He said that the green treeless hills made him think of New Zealand: "They could have filmed *Lord of the Rings* here." He pointed out the surrounding mountains—Adams looming to the south and Rainier to the North. "Misty Mountains. Mountains of Moria. I loved those movies," he said.

"I've been to New Zealand," I said. "This looks more like Australia."

Mitch laughed and gave me the look, the same look other car salesman give me, the one that says, "Go away. The men are talking."

"How do you folks feel about a little drive? Maybe I can give you a quick feel for the area." Winston accepted. "We'll swing past the cancer center first," said Mitch, "and then maybe we can look at some houses—just to get a sense of what's available."

Mitch drove us past the airport and down 40th Avenue. He pointed to the newly built dental and physical therapy centers. He showed us a golf course across from a high school. There were blocks of small rambler houses, all of them looking as if they were built in the Kennedy administration, and then a small shopping center. Mitch said, "The Walgreen's new." He went on about recent development. "They just added a Wal-Mart, if you like that sort of thing. It was very controversial for a while. Now there are Wal-Marts on both the east and west side of Yakima."

Not a selling point.

Past the bank and an assisted living center was the cancer

center. Mitch said that it was only a few years old and was a state-of-the-art facility. "I'm really looking forward to having you meet the doctors," he said. "If I ever get cancer, there's no place I'd rather go, than here." As if all doctors were oncologists.

The building looked like it had been designed by Jackson Hole architects fashioning a hospital from of a lodge. "It's 42,000 square feet, built on five acres, and has a stream flowing through it," Mitch said. Perhaps he had spent time in real estate. "Waterfalls, natural stone and rock landscaping, and comforting earth tones."

Mitch drove us past some churches, by a skate park and soccer fields. He toured along Scenic Drive, a strip of garish hilltop homes inspired by *Miami Vice* reruns.

"Where's the shopping," I asked. "Where's the center?"

"Yakima has many centers." Mitch described pockets of culture and commerce. He said that the only way to really know Yakima was to live in Yakima, to be part of the community. He said, "Seattle has obvious culture. But Yakima is more personal. It's community."

Give me obvious.

Mitch drove north, past a little cowboy town called Selah. He took a country road and tried, once again, to sell us on the hills. "Look at them. Look at those mountains behind them. If only we had more time, I could show you the rivers, the fields, the orchards," said Mitch. "We could take a little drive and see Mount Saint Helens or go to Maryhill. They have Rodins there. I know it's no Museum of Fine Arts, but it's still amazing."

The road followed the Yakima River as it cut between Mitch's beloved hills. He pointed to an enclave of newer large homes nestled into the slopes. He said that one of the Mahre twins built a dream house above the man-made pond. "D'you know Phil and Steve Mahre—the slalom skiing brothers that won gold and silver in the '80s?"

"It's beautiful out here," said Winston.

"Well, I'm sure, if you're interested, we could find you a home nearby."

"I'm not living on a farm," I said.

Mitch whispered something to Winston about knowing some good agents then turned the car around, back toward Yakima. He pointed to fly fishermen on the river. "Ever do any fishing, Dr. Townsend?" he asked.

"Call me Winston," he said. "And no, not for a while."

"Let me know if you want to give it a go," said the salesman. "I have an extra rod. We can get you a license easy."

For a moment I thought Winston was seriously considering the flabby man's offer. I reminded him of his allergies and the time he slipped a disk playing golf.

"I'm being so rude," said Mitch. "You folks have flown across country, travelled in a cramped jet, and I'm hauling you around the outback. You probably want a chance to get to your hotel and settle in."

"No hurry," said Winston—a doctor with bedside manner humoring the pathetic beast. He could probably smell the lung cancer on Mitch's breath.

"The hotel would be nice," I said, saving Winston from another hour of hills and houses. Mitch drove back on the freeway and motioned to the left side of the road. He told us about the Greenway, a paved walking path flowing parallel to the Yakima River. "Can you fish there?" said Winston.

"Sure. Mostly, it's just a place to walk or ride bikes.

Sometimes I take the kids and we just go down the path and throw rocks into the river."

I pointed to a billboard on the side of the road. "What's that?"

"Ah, yes," said Mitch. "That sign is famous."

Winston looked out his window and squinted to read: "Welcome to Yakima, the Palm Springs of Washington." The billboard was ridiculous, like someone with a spare Saturday, extra housepaint, and a junior high art class put it together. The *Yakima* section was centered on the sign in some old-west-saloon typeface, and *The Palm Springs* ascended in a slate green script. Then the of *Washington* was tagged on in red paint with that same saloon font. Three apples were in the top corner, like a parody of Classical Greek genitalia.

"What does that even mean?" I said.

"That sign's been around for twenty-five years," said Mitch. "It's meant to say that Yakima is a little paradise with lots of sunshine."

"Why not choose a better place, like comparing to San Jose or San Diego?"

"I don't know, Mrs. Townsend," said Mitch. "Palm Springs just seems to have a little glamour to it, I guess."

"Have you ever been to Palm Springs?" I said. "They elected Sonny Bono mayor."

"Yakima has its own celebrities," said Mitch and threw out a shortlist of memorized names: Kyle MacLachlan, Sam Kinison, Beverly Cleary, and Dave Edler.

I didn't know any of them except Cleary and MacLachlan. My Cuban roommate loved Twin Peaks.

"Lee Ermey?" said Winston.

"The Gunnery Sergeant from *Full Metal Jacket*," said Mitch. "Y'know, the one who says, 'Outstanding, Private Pyle.'" Winston, for whatever reason, and with the sort of vulgarity that I had only seen twice in our marriage—neither time sober—shouted out with a horrid southern accent, "God has a hard-on for Marines because we kill everything we see."

Mitch, before I could apologize, trumped Winston's crudity: "What is your major malfunction, numb nuts?"

"Sound off like you got a pair," said Winston, aping some faux-American South dialect.

"The first and the last word out of your filthy sewers will be 'Sir.' Do you maggots understand that?"

"So you can give your heart to Jesus, but your ass belongs to the Corps."

"Winston," I said. The car quieted and I could only think how right I was to come. Mitch cast a spell on my poor husband, a stunting, testosterone-filled trance that made a professional man act like a frat house bartender.

Mitch took the exit and drove us toward the hotel, a modest but, relative to what Mitch had showed us, attractive building. Mitch told us how the Hilton formed the center of the downtown revitalization project and that there was still a pulse in the heart of the town. He pulled along the street and parked. He opened my door as if a small gesture of civility would hide his basic brutishness. He fetched our luggage from the trunk. "We'll get you checked in. If you like, I'd be happy to take you out to dinner," he said. "An Olive Garden is a block that way, and, just past that, on this side of the street, is Santiago's. Fantastic Mexican."

Winston walked to the back of the car to help with the bags, but Mitch insisted on carrying everything. So, my dear husband, accustomed to helping, consoled the ruddy man and asked what his nights were made of, what Mitch-the-headhunter did to keep alive in his village.

"I'll be honest with you folks," he said, as he wheezed from the combination of obesity and manual labor. "We don't do much at night. But my family lives here and we see each other most nights. We go to parks or walk around Costco eating samples. Sometimes we sit around watching TV on Saturdays. We have church on Sundays. I never get stuck in traffic, and I've never been shot. I could tell you what I do with the hospital, but it's not worth talking about, and my job is to give you something to talk about. But that's how home is." The big ox took a deep breath as we reached the front counter. He was sweating. "They'll take care of you here."

A hotel employee came to the counter and took our bags. Mitch handed him a card and a ten-dollar bill. Then he reached into his coat pocket and produced an envelope with our room number, two pass cards, and a gift certificate for some local bar. "My card's in there if you need anything."

I bid a gracious farewell and turned my attention to the lobby. Winston shook Mitch's hand again and said something about fishing—always the peacemaker, that man. "Anytime," said Mitch. "I keep an extra rod locked-and-loaded at all times."

"It's probably too late now," said Winston.

"It's never too late for fishing, if you don't mind me bringing my oldest."

Winston looked at me, as if—for some reason—I had ceased to be his wife and had become his mother. His eyes, those full brown eyes that first drew me to him, asked me if I would permit him to play in the water with the salesman. Sometimes he was such a child. But fishing was the perfect thing for Winston at that moment. Not because it would ignite some primal maleness, but because it would say why Yakima was wrong more clearly than any opinion I could offer. Winston wasn't some western pioneer, a Meriwether Lewis moving between peaks and valleys seeking a hidden passage to the Pacific. Winston Townsend was a respected heart doctor, a bureaucrat, a man who thought Land's End blazers were too rustic. After an hour in weeds and waders, he would limp back to the car and beg for a seafood restaurant and a gin and tonic. And Mitch, that bumbling hustler, would probably pump Winston full of deep-fried hot dogs and Budweiser until Winston felt ill, overwhelmed and malnourished.

"Yes, go fishing Winston," I said. I followed the clerk and the bags and smiled, picturing my husband with the fat man out on the river. By nightfall, Winston would beg for civilization.

NIGHTSTAND
66TH AVE AND ENGLEWOOD

On the night of his death, Brian was thirsty. Julie filled a glass and brought it to bed. Brian left the glass, one sip left, on the nightstand he and Julie received on their wedding day eight years earlier.

The nightstand was a gift from Julie's mother. It was an heirloom Julie's maternal grandmother had brought with her when emigrating from Sweden: a standard Gustavian knockoff that filled the homes of the poor—painted white and garnished with gold lines that had chipped and fragmented like elided sentences.

A year after Brian and Julie's wedding, Julie's cousin Meg visited the house. Meg saw the nightstand and accused Julie of stealing it. She believed the furniture was expensive because it was old. But after consulting an antique dealer and a lawyer—a friend of the family—Meg did not mention the nightstand again. No one in the family did.

Meg never again visited Brian and Julie, not even for the baptism of their daughter, Emily, who was a week away from her fourth birthday and—for that night—at her grandmother's. Emily didn't know yet.

Julie thought about these things. She thought about how she would someday pass the nightstand on to Emily. Years after she told Emily about Brian, silent beside her. Long after the water in the glass had evaporated.

THE THINGS LEFT BEHIND
AT MYTHIC RECORDS, 1982–2011
9TH AVE AND SUMMITVIEW

Yes, Pearl Jam and Radiohead loved LPs. But vinyl was for the hipsters, the people who showed up once a year on Record Store Day for a collectible Clash repressing. But CDs hadn't sold in five years. Digital had won. Streaming had forced Mythic Records into a mass grave with the mid-size newspapers, specialty bookstores, and other ruins of twentieth-century commerce. The store's shelves were museum pieces, stocked with vestiges of '70s post-punk, '80s pop, '90s grunge, and "aughtie's" hip hop.

On this, the final day of a record store that was—like the rock star who bought and named it—a local legend, Daniel LeBarnes remained to inventory and liquidate his inheritance. He shuffled through the stacks. Dusty Springfield. Rick Springfield. The Springfields. He pulled out Springsteen's *Nebraska* and set it on a pile near a Ringo Starr life-size cardboard cutout. He gathered the remaining records into a box and wrote *SELL* with a Sharpie. He sealed the box with packing tape and lugged it to the front counter.

The brick walls were stripped except for promotional posters that wouldn't sell and decals that wouldn't move. The likenesses of Eminem and Britney Spears formed a permanent truce, each bound by nails to the mortar. The Mother Love

Bone bumper sticker held to the front door. It would be there forever, like the Melvins concert flyer glued to the register. These would be artifacts left for the new residents: a seasonal gift store called Holly, Jolly & Folly (boxes of skeletons and musical tombstones were already in the backroom waiting for Halloween).

Daniel had run Mythic Records for the last fifteen years, something of a family business. Before him, his mother, Leah, managed the whole thing. It was her alimony. And she was, by default, a minor celebrity.

"Yes," she told customers, "*That* Andy LeBarnes." She meant the Andy LeBarnes who fronted Fantastic Voyage. The Andy LeBarnes who opened for Roxy Music and almost bested Robert Palmer to become the frontman of The Power Station. The Andy LeBarnes who hadn't been to Yakima in fourteen years (the last time he had seen Daniel). The Andy LeBarnes who wrote "Mythic Mama (I Love to Love You)" about her.

> *Babe, I can see you under the stones / I can hear the ancient drama,*
> *You bring me back to home / I love to love you,*
> *Mythic Mama.*

"You're Mythic Mama," the customers said.

"Yes," said Leah.

At the other end of the store, Larry Masini, Mythic Record's last employee, boxed discs. Larry was an amalgam of retro-minimalist fashions: James Dean meets Nick Cave meets Glenn Danzig. Buddy Holly glasses. White T-shirt. Black Levis. Oxblood Doc Martens. The cigarettes (soft pack Camels) were rolled into his right sleeve. Larry should have been Andy and

Leah LeBarnes's son. Larry looked and lived the part. Not like Daniel. Daniel didn't even smoke. Daniel preferred Gap over vintage clothing, romantic comedies over horror, and early-to-bed evenings over pot-drenched afterparties. And then there was his taste in music.

Daniel, given the right amount of torture, would confess to hating Bob Dylan, the stuff that currently saturated the building (it being Larry's turn to choose music). If pressed, he might say Pink Floyd was overrated and Van Halen was better with Sammy Hagar. If heavily intoxicated, he could even admit his weakness for Swedish dance bands. In a moment of trust and vulnerability—perhaps on a tenth wedding anniversary, should he ever marry—he might show his closet collection of ABBA 45s, his set of unmailed Roxette postage stamps, his signed Robyn press photo. Maybe it was his fault the store went under. He lacked the facial lines, the rehab stories, the uninhibited libido.

Larry, using both hands, ran a black unbreakable comb through his greased ebony hair as if primping for a Joey Ramone costume party. "Smoke break," he said. He turned the knob with his left forearm, opened the door with his elbow, and held it with his foot as he lit his Zippo. The brass bell rang. *Ping.* For thirty years, that bell announced the entrances and exits of Mythic Records' citizens.

Daniel stopped Dylan. This was his last chance to evoke the Mythic Records Break Law:

> Section 1. Any Mythic Records employee
> controlling the store sound system surrenders
> his or her authority upon vacating store
> premises for any reason—cigarettes, cell

phones, or coffee—for any amount of time, so long as he or she *completely* (i.e., both feet outside the door) exits the building.

Section 2. The employee nearest the sound system is required to exchange the vacating employee's music for more desirable music ("desirable" is defined as any music that the employee nearest the sound system likes more).

Section 3. The returning employee must silently endure the new music with the understanding that eventually the newest custodian will require food, vice, and/or a toilet (see Section 1).

Daniel pulled *Blood on the Tracks* and inserted *Autobahn*. The Law—the constant change of music—meant that Mythic Records was always new. An exchange of polycarbonate plastic discs changed a singer-songwriter's weathered philosophy into Kraftwerk's German-Euro techno industrial kitsch. It changed an artistically conscious indie shop into an unintentionally ironic nostalgia haven.

In two weeks, those same speakers will spew "Monster Mash." In two months, they will run a constant loop of Peggy Lee, Garth Brooks, and Bing Crosby singing "White Christmas," the official anthem of Purgatory (where it's always December 23). Daniel will leave the sound system. It was as much a part of the building as the plumbing.

But first, the shelves needed to be cleared of their other holdings: a Star Trek bong from a Blind Melon concert, a headless George Harrison figurine Daniel's dad said belonged to Eric Clapton, the top-shelf Madonna cone bra covered in dust. With a puff of canned air, Daniel blew the sediment from the relics and sorted them on the front counter. Right side: storage. Left side: eBay.

◆

On the third shelf, a "Stevie Nicks Is A Witch" pentagram necklace draped over it, was the high school graduation night photo: just Daniel and Leah (Andy somewhere on tour, living in London by then).

That graduation night Daniel went to Burger Ranch with Leah. It was their place. They had eaten there every other Thursday since he could remember. When he had braces and Leah took him out of school for orthodontist appointments, they would always stop there on the way home, and they would sit in one of the yellow and brown booths and talk, he with his banana milkshake and crinkle fries, she with her Bushwhack Burger and Coke. They thought it normal for middle-aged mothers and teen rock-star offspring to enjoy one another.

On Graduation Night, they were both ready to celebrate. They smiled about the future, but not the same future. Daniel tapped his feet, anxious to announce leaving for England to live with his dad for a while—a ticket for London, Andy's graduation present, was in Daniel's left rear pocket. Leah stirred the ice in her Coke.

"What do you think about Europe?" Daniel said.

Leah chewed. She set her burger on its yellow wrapper, wiped her fingertips, and looked out the window like she was trying to make out the specials at the deli across the street. "I don't know," she said. "I've never gone."

"You went with Dad, right?" he said. "They loved him there."

"I think the first summer, the year before you were born, maybe I should have gone with him. He came back crazy and excited, and I tried to be excited for him. He kept talking about how wonderful Europe was and that 'In Europe, it's not like here.'"

"You should've gone."

"It changed him," she said. "Which I guess is normal, right? A cliché? The small-town boy comes back with glitter under one eye."

"But you could've gone," said Daniel.

"Your father said an orchardist's daughter would never understand Europe."

"But he's from Yakima," said Daniel.

"The universe's accident. Becoming a rock star corrected that."

"But he wrote the song about you."

"He wrote it a week after you were born. On tour, in Europe. Maybe he was right."

"About?"

"Maybe I didn't understand it all, because I would've rather had him here than be called 'Mythic Mama.' I mean, who doesn't want to be some girl who gets to be eternally young?"

So Daniel dipped his fries in pink sauce, a mix of mayonnaise and ketchup. He and Leah talked about high school and that they should close the store for a week and take a road trip to Yosemite. They talked about community college and how Daniel could still work at the store while he went to school and, maybe, when he was finished, if he wanted to, he could manage.

◆

The bell ping signaled Larry's return. "What the—?" said Larry. Larry generally disregarded the "silently endure" clause of the Break Law.

"Without Kraftwerk," said Daniel, "there's no Moby, no Chemical Brothers."

"I want to live in that world," said Larry.

Larry surveyed Daniel's new piles. "Can I have this?" He lifted a ZZ Top keychain. Daniel nodded. Larry stacked and rummaged through the memorabilia as Daniel retrieved it from the shelves. Devo cone hat. *eBay*. Nancy Wilson guitar strap. *Storage*. Hip-shaking Elvis clock. *eBay*. Larry formed his own pile of embezzled novelties: the Corey Hart sunglasses, the Jefferson Airplane incense holder.

Daniel didn't take everything. He didn't bother with the leftovers from previous owners, from Mr. Winters who owned Mythic Records under the name Sun City Sounds. In a cubby toward the top, a pincushion hid behind a Rolodex. They were leftovers from Kraft's Big Body clothing store. When Andy and Leah bought the place, they found carbon pads from Jim's Stitch & Sew and receipts from Marilynn's Fine Floral. The building hid recesses and false walls waiting to be discovered by a contractor or curious boy, and Daniel imagined that some future owner would stumble upon a hidden safe or a skull in a basement cupboard. It was Daniel's duty to leave things behind. Failure to do so was like breaking a cosmic chain letter. He dropped personalized pens behind the backroom lockers and guitar picks in the air vents.

Daniel climbed a stepladder for one final scan. He took what he wanted. He removed items of embarrassment or questionable legality. Only the debris on the top shelf remained: a bunch of dried carnations, a hacky sack, and a metal box propping up the Madonna bra.

Larry dropped a Paul McCartney Christmas ornament. It didn't break. *eBay.*

Daniel brought the box down, a possible cache of forgotten fortune left by the old pop star or government bonds overlooked by Mr. Winters. He dusted the box. It was the kind used for taking tickets at high school football games: plain, slate gray, adorned only by a plastic handle, a tin clasp, and a silver lock. Papers shifted inside.

Daniel walked the box to a bare space on the counter.

"Whatcha find?" said Larry.

Daniel flipped the clasp. The cover refused to budge. The lock, still faithful.

"I'll get a hammer," said Larry. He hurried toward the backroom.

"A screwdriver, too. A flathead." Daniel shook the box. He looked for signs of ownership or usage. The box was silent. Kraftwerk pulsed on.

"This song, man." Larry handed the tools to Daniel.

Daniel slid the screwdriver into a seam. He made a few failed attacks before the box yielded, revealing stacks of ivory and eggshell colored envelopes. They were set vertically, dozens of them—some torn at the top, others split with a letter opener, and a few that looked unopened.

"Money?" said Larry. He ran his right hand against his hair, restoring it to conformity. "Maybe this is the movie ending, right? The store is run out of business but is miraculously saved by an inheritance?"

"Doubt it," said Daniel.

Each envelope was hand addressed: flowing cursive letters, some in India Ink. Several had been mailed, posted to Andy LeBarnes, care of Enterprise Management, Lakewood, California. They had cancelled British postage. They all originated from J. Susan, London.

Larry and Daniel each grabbed a half-dozen envelopes.

"Dear Andy," began Larry:

> I miss you. I'm so tired of the road and the endless evenings of crowds that don't want me. They want Bowie in tight suits and glitter surrounded by girls who will show their breasts. I stand up there in black and they think I'm a freak. I love the way you listen. You see me.

"Andy, my love," read Daniel:

> I was back in London for a few weeks and it's so different now. Why should it be strange to me? I've lived here all my life and now I can't recognize it.

They thumbed through the letters. Each began with similar salutations: "Dear Andy," "Dearest Andy," "Andy, my beautiful." They were signed *Janet* or *JS* or *J.* Thinking of you, Janet. Love, JS. Your eternal love, J.

"Isn't your mom's name, Leah?"

Daniel didn't answer.

"Player," said Larry. "Want coffee? I'll get coffee."

Ping.

◆

Daniel held the cashbox against his ribs. He walked past the dimly lit hallway as sounds of passing BMWs and Mercedes ran through the speakers, driving in time to perfectly coordinated beats and synthesizer tones. Daniel set the box and the letters on his oak desk, a desk older than him, perhaps older than his parents. He opened another letter.

Daniel had already archived the desk's contents, its fifteen years of office supplies and nostalgia. The leftover Post-it pads, the capless pens, the receipts and invoices now filed in the trash. The dearest remnants—the FedEx stress ball, the UPS coffee mug, the Swingline stapler— found their way to a Chiquita banana box sitting near the cashbox. The essential icons of Daniel and Leah LeBarnes sat atop it all: A signed CD of *Druid*, Fantastic Voyage's most famous album.

Daniel didn't hear the ping, but he noticed the momentary silence and then the new music: synthesizers and guitars and crooning of a band he had always treasured but could never publicly claim, not while trying to run an independent music store.

Larry, the darkened, stylized agent of vintage pop culture, emerged into the office. He set a white cup with grease pencil markings onto Daniel's desk between the two boxes, near the growing stack of envelopes.

"Is it 'modren' or' modern'?"

"Modren," said Daniel. "'I am the *modren* man.' I have no

idea what it means."

"I don't think it's a word."

"Styx?"

"It's all that's left," said Larry. "Consider it a compromise. They at least have guitars."

Daniel went to the stack on his desk and grabbed a letter from the middle of the pile. "Here's an early one," he said.

July 31, 1974

Dear Andy,

I don't usually write these sort of letters, but I had to let you know how much fun I had in Liverpool. I've been there dozens of times but never with people who have such romantic thoughts about that dingy town. I forget how important the idea of Liverpool is.

Thinking of you, Janet.

"Not too bad," said Larry.

"A month later," said Daniel.

August 23, 1974

My Sweet Andy,

I've enjoyed our time together and can't stand the idea of you leaving for Berlin. I wish you would stay longer—there's so much more to see here, although I prefer the time when I'm not playing the tour guide (not that I don't enjoy that, too). I already miss your warmth and your humor and your wonderful eyes.

Missing you, Janet.

"It's just fan stuff," said Larry. "This Janet bird is blinded by spandex." Larry grabbed letters and sat down on his own emptied desk, a small table he used for storing his cigarettes.

They took turns reading to each other, reading as Janet

moved from talking about England and touring in 1974, to professions of love in 1975, to questions of how long it would be until Andy finally decided—until Andy finally stayed for longer than a tour. The earliest letters were about how wonderful it was for Janet to talk with Andy: he understood her. The later letters were yearnings: *we can't deny our love anymore; your sweet spirit will be divided as long as your heart and his body are divided.* The letters from 1977 lost their lyricism. They were blunt pleas: *I miss you* and *when will you decide* and *maybe I should come to the States.*

"Here's the thing," said Larry. "Your dad was at the top then. He should have at least been with Siouxsie Sioux or Chrissie Hynde."

"Not helping," said Daniel.

Daniel started another: "I am so happy. I felt so free in Wilshire—"

Daniel stopped. He scanned ahead, silently, as Larry listened for Janet's great new experience, but Daniel didn't speak it. He handed the letter to Larry.

Larry read it. He exhaled. He tucked it back into its envelope and returned it to Daniel.

"Damn," said Larry.

"Yep."

"Three days after I was born," said Daniel.

"Three days."

Daniel gathered the letters, all but that last one, and returned them to the cashbox. He stood and he took that letter, that truth that he was never supposed to know, and he placed it into his back pocket. The muffled sounds of "Heavy Metal Poisoning" weaved into the back room.

"Do you think your Mom?" asked Larry. And he asked *who put the letters up there* and *do you think they're worth anything* and *are you going to talk to your Mom about them* and *what about your Dad* and *do you think he and this Janet bird stayed together* and *what do you do with them now.*

"I don't know," said Daniel.

"I'm going to finish up out front," said Larry.

Larry had somehow endured the ongoing stream of ballads, rockers, and concept songs, all merged onto *Kilroy Was Here*, a forty-minute encapsulation of all that was right and wrong with 1983 rock music. Maybe the music made him work faster. He dumped the garbage, removed his embezzled memorabilia, and drew a Sharpie unibrow on Britney Spears.

Daniel returned to the counter. "Sorry I took so long," he said.

"No problem. I put your stuff in your car," said Larry.

"Nice."

"And the letters?"

"More of the same," said Daniel.

Larry formed a sound—something of a grunt. He stepped toward Daniel for what could have turned into a hug or a back pat or a fist bump. He stopped short. An invisible heterosexual barrier prevented touch. "I'll take the truck to the unit and unload. You can say your goodbyes."

Daniel tapped his knuckles on the glass countertop.

Larry pulled a "Frankie Says Relax" bumper sticker from the eBay pile, peeled it, and slammed it to the middle of the front window.

"Hey Larry," said Daniel. "It's been good working with you."

Larry nodded. He said, "I stole a box of Halloween candy from the back room."

Ping.

Daniel took a partially-filled black plastic bag from the counter. He walked back to the office, past the boxes, direct from China, of Holly, Jolly & Folly merchandise. He went to his desk and the lock box and tossed the box and its artifacts into the bag with the unwanted debris: the Flavor Flav neck clock, the John Lennon nude photo, the David Lee Roth sweatband. He tied the bag and walked it to the alley dumpster. He returned for his Chiquita box, checked the backroom for anything forgotten, flushed the toilet, and flicked off the back lights.

Daniel went back behind the counter, standing face to face with the stereo, the heart and voice of Mythic Records. He ejected the disc, interrupting a third pass through an imaginary rock opera. He pulled his copy of the Fantastic Voyage CD, his only record of Andy's voice, from the banana box and set *Druid* on the barren shelf, the stones and trees artwork face down. He inserted the disc into the stereo tray and pressed a white triangle on a black, beveled button. Andy LeBarnes's voice— pathetically dated—filled the room for the first time in at least a decade.

Babe, I can see you under the stones/ I can hear the ancient drama.

Daniel heard—he swore he heard—a voice behind him. It was singing or talking or breathing in time with Andy's vocals. Daniel faced the north wall, aware for the first time how red— how iron red—the bricks were. The voice carried on, more a feeling than a sound, flowing from the envelope in Daniel's rear pocket.

June 27, 1975

Dearest Andy,

I am so happy. I felt so free in Wiltshire, like we were released from all the dogmas and rules of thousands of years of religion and war and emotional rubbish put on us by people who are afraid to be happy. It was like we were those ancients with painted faces and open clothes and hearts. And I saw you watching me dancing behind those stone pillars. We were like beautiful stories and we were ancient too, like the stones. We were part of some great myth that people will tell.

Your eternal goddess, J.

Daniel pulled the envelope from his pocket and folded it. He set his foot on the second shelf and lifted himself. With his left hand, he gripped the upper shelf. With his right he reached behind the Rolodex and the pincushion. He wedged the folded envelope into the corner.

Returning to the ground, Daniel pressed the "repeat" button on the stereo. He placed the Styx CD into the banana box, in the space left open by his father's album. He stepped out from behind the counter and ran his left hand across the brick walls. He walked past the street-side windows to the glass door and stood on an old footstool and pulled down the brass bell. He walked the bell back to the banana box, lifted the box, and exited Mythic Records. Everything else, he left behind.

HOMECOMING
17TH AVE AND TAHOMA

The soldiers shuffled within the plane, trying to keep order in themselves as they had tried to keep it over "there." They descended the stairs and stepped onto America. They faced, across the airfield, the wives and children they were ordered to leave a year before.

When the order came, the soldiers broke their ranks and rushed to their wives. The wives split the tape and ran to their husbands. As the two sides closed, the soldiers saw that their wives were not as beautiful as they had remembered, and the wives forgot why they needed their men. But neither could stop the momentum of joyous reunion.

BIRTHDAY
YAKIMA AVE AND FRONT

I love Kim, I really do. But if she flirts with that damned waiter one more time, I'll scream. If anyone gets the man, it should be me. Kim's already gone through two husbands and this is my birthday—and not just any birthday, but that horrible, life-ending fortieth. And I don't mind being single, but some nights I need to forget my only comforts are two puppies and worknight drinks with the girls.

The whole mess starts early. There are three of us at Tequila's, but you would never know that from the waiter. The only reason he acknowledges me is because Kim says I'm the birthday girl, which means I will end the evening in a sombrero. And Mindy. Sometimes even I forget about Mindy. That poor woman was born to be overlooked. Even I, not the most beautiful flower in the bouquet, wouldn't wear a "World's Greatest" anything shirt outside the flower garden.

Kim raises her hand and waives to the waiter, a Latino Sean Connery, who stops talking to a guy in a business suit. He has no choice but to come—no man does around Kim.

His white shirt is crisp and clean. Kim, I can see it in her posture, wants to crumple it.

"Buenos tardes señoritas," he says, and his for-show Spanish makes me feel like a tourist. He switches to the business language of these Mexican-American restaurants and asks, in English, if we want to start with drinks.

"I shouldn't drink tonight," I say.

"Oh please, woman," says Kim. "As if. I'm not drinking alone."

"I'll drive you home if you want something," says Mindy, being helpful, I'm sure.

"There you go," says Kim. She turns to the waiter. "I would love a banana margarita."

"Y por tú? Que desea tomar?" he says.

"Sólo una Coca Cola," I say.

"Hell no. She'll have a strawberry margarita," says Kim.

"Yes, strawberry and banana," says the waiter. "Those are lovely flavors—very adventurous." Mindy asks for glass of water. "Agua. Bien."

"Would you ladies like anything else?"

Kim giggles with the subtlety of a prostitute. She puts her hand on the waiter's elbow. "What's your name?"

"Felix."

"Just drinks, Felix. For now." Kim tilts her head and flashes her newly whitened teeth, all tricks she learned from her long-lost youth in the pageantry circuit. Felix leaves for the kitchen. Kim watches him. "Nice ass. And no ring."

"Maybe he had a ring on his right hand," says Mindy. "Isn't it right hand in Mexico?"

"That's Germany," says Kim.

"I think he's Argentinean," I say.

Kim says, "Who cares?"

"I know a perfect guy for you, Bea," says Kim.

Kim has names for her shoes. She can describe where they came from. There's an ancestry for her black pumps. For all I care, they're from Payless. They look nice, and that's what counts. But not to Kim. I've known her to drive to Portland for the right shoes. If she were only as choosy about her men.

"I don't trust your 'perfect guys,'" I say. "Remember that guy, Richard, you set me up with? He asked me to go down on him on the first date."

"Did you?"

"I have a cousin in Selah," says Mindy. Even Mindy the church girl is helpless in Kim's presence. When it's just the two of us, she never talks about men. Tonight, she's cupid.

"Is this the contractor? The bald guy?" says Kim. "He's the one that drove into the florist shop, right?"

"He's a good guy," says Mindy. "He had some problems with his ex-wife, but they've worked that out and she moved back to Nebraska. He put his life in order. He started going to church. Hasn't even had a drink in nine months. Besides, he actually looks younger now that he shaved his head and grew the goatee."

"That reminds me, Kim," I say. "You remember Meg from high school—the pastor's daughter?"

"You'd like her, Min," says Kim.

"She's splitting up with Paul. Unbelievable—after eighteen years. It makes you doubt everything, like if Paul and Meg can't make it, maybe it's better to be single. If you're single, you don't walk in on your husband...." I cut myself off, but it's too late. It only takes a whiff of gossip to make Kim salivate.

"Walk in on what? What'd he do?"

"I shouldn't say," I say.

"Bea, you slut," says Kim. "You brought it up. You have to finish it."

I leaned into the table. Kim glistens. I say, "He was, um, pleasuring himself."

"Shit, that's nothing," says Kim. She pulls away and adjusts her breasts. "He's a guy. That's what guys do. That's like divorcing a guy for farting."

"He was doing that while," and I lean in again. Kim, unable to resist, shoves her chest and arms on the table and pulls in close enough to kiss me. I wonder.

She stays low, as if she intends to lick the salsa from the middle of the table. Her gold cross falls into the tortilla chips. "He did it while watching guys on his computer."

"Shit." Kim repeats her favorite word. "Gay porn? Really?"

"Yeah, lots of it. You know Meg, right? Beautiful. Perfect," I say. "There's Meg. And Paul has a thing for guys. She found magazines in his desk and some plastic toys."

"Toys? What kind of toys?" says Mindy.

"He had a hard drive full of pictures."

Kim laughs, leans back in her chair, and laughed again. "So Paul's a fag?"

"Really, Kim," says Mindy. "That word is so offensive."

"So is pretending your wife is Clay Aiken."

"There's a program at our church," says Mindy. "It's supposed to help gay people become straight."

I can't help wondering how something like that works. In our family, there is no such thing as being gay. We never talk about it. Growing up, my parents sent me to my room whenever I asked about Aunt Alicia and her roommate, Tina.

"Paul says he's not gay, just curious," I say.

"What about Meg?" says Mindy.

"She wants out. She said he violated their covenant marriage. It's against God's order and all that."

"Makes sense," says Mindy.

"Gay must be the new mid-life crisis," says Kim.

"Poor Meg," says Mindy.

Felix returns with an armful of glasses and an introductory Spanish class. "Fresa for the señorita on her twenty-first birthday." "El plátano for the beauty." Kim beams over the yellow slush as if it were liquid youth. "Agua." He asks if we are ready to order. He didn't bring a pad or pencil. He only repeats: "Arroz con pollo. Arroz con pollo. And for you?"

"Taco salad" I say. "No guacamole."

"Oh, no guacamole on mine either," says Mindy. She tugs her shirt as it had bunched around her belly. Kim tells Mindy she should join the gym with her. She says that Mindy could look pretty if she loses some weight and fixes her hair.

"I thought you liked guacamole," I say.

"She likes it too much," says Kim.

The margarita isn't Kim's worst idea. It gives me something to work on while Kim rants about work and Bob, our boss, and how he is losing his hair and "like just shave it, already." She asks if I think Mitch in packaging is cute. "He asked me to go with him to Vegas in March," she says.

Mindy's great, but she's absolutely worthless on nights like this. When the food comes out, she just grazes on it, afraid that

Kim will rip on her weight. "Did you use enough sour cream?" says Kim.

Felix checks on us—on Kim—four times while we eat. He brings fresh chips and refills our margaritas. Kim even gets him to sit on her lap and test out her third drink. "I think it's a little weak," she says. "You tell me if there's enough in it."

"I'll get you a new one," he says. "I'll make it myself."

"Kim," I say. "You're the only person I know whose boobs point up."

Felix takes our plates away and offers to box Mindy's food. Min looks at Kim and says she doesn't need to take it home.

"I hope it was good," says Felix.

"Yes, almost too good," say Mindy. "Maybe you can box it and I'll save it for my husband."

Kim tugs on Felix's black pants. He leaned into her as she whispers into his ear. "Un momento," he says and takes away our empty glasses.

Felix returns with a trio of waiters and a plate of flan. They sing a royalty-free form of "Happy Birthday" as one of the kitchen staff sets a grotesque black circle on my head. Mindy and Kim clap like eight year-olds. After the song, Felix shouts, "Feliz cumpleaños," and sets the plate of flan-with-a-candle in front of me, then stands next to Kim.

"Happy Birthday, Beatrice," says Mindy. "Make a wish. Blow it out." I stare at the orange square. In my whole life—and my parents were first generation—I can't remember ever making flan. They like cake in Mexico.

This is all part of Kim's trap. She is now the good friend, the one who provided drinks and flan for her flabby-forty-year-old co-worker. She leans her head onto Felix's arm and I do my best not to spit. No one looks good blowing out a birthday candle. And the sombrero, even Kim couldn't pull off wearing that monstrosity.

Mindy and the staff clap as I puff. "Nice blow," says Kim. Her hand moves up Felix's leg.

"What'd you wish for?" says Mindy.

Kim is still alive. Such is the wish-granting power of flan.

The staff walks away, leaving me with the sombrero, the unnatural dessert, and the girls.

"I'll be right back," says Kim. "I just have to check something on the bill."

"That's such a cute hat," says Mindy.

"You should wear it."

I hand it to her and she puts it on her head and says, "Hola." Then she tries to hand it back. "I'm sorry. I don't mean to be offensive."

"Don't worry Mindy. You have a long way to go before you offend."

Kim returns and pulls the hair back from her face. She unwraps a mint and hands two more to us. "I got the bill paid," she says.

"Wow," says Mindy. "That's wonderful."

"Yes, Kim. You're a wonderful person," I say.

"Hey, Min. Do you mind driving Bea home?"

Mindy says she already planned on driving all of us home, but Kim says she's going to stay a while. "Felix gets off at ten. He said he could give me a lift."

"I thought you gave the lifts," I say. Kim flips me off, kisses me on the forehead, and disappears into the bathroom.

Mindy asks if she can try the flan. "I've never had flan." I give her the plate. "I know it's not my night," she says, "but this was a pretty great birthday."

"Yes, Mindy," I say. "A dream come true."

BORDERS
NACHES AVE AND FAIR

I know Miguel didn't hate white people. His buyers were white. Anna was white. It wasn't about skin color. It was about loyalty and respect. Maybe Anna understood that at first. She was there for Miguel, and when she forgot, Miguel reminded her. And if she didn't remember after that, Miguel said he'd send her back to her parents in West Valley so they could put her in rehab and take her to some nice church and make her date a cowboy and pretend like she never had a baby with a Mexican.

But Anna could be loyal, like after Guero got shot when the cops came looking for us, and Anna acted like a regular white girl, like on TV, and she asked for a search warrant and shit. She said she needed to call her lawyer before they could come inside, and the whole time me and Miguel were crawling out the bathroom window. I think Anna stayed around because she loved the *chiva*, that nasty black shit and the needles. She knew that if she went back to West Valley, her parents would make her give it up and go to school and then she would have to get a job in the Valley Mall or Goodwill until her arms healed up.

I remember that Saturday. Ever since I've been locked up, it's all I think about. Time is all I have, and time is all I'll ever have, and I'm cool with that. There's no future here, just the past, like living in a picture. No one ever says, "What do you do?" like I have a job or some shit. It's always, "What *did* you do?"

Me and Miguel were at the apartment and he was all in a hurry and started fucking with me because I was fixing my hair, going on about being pretty and shit. But he shut up because the baby was crying. So he went into the bedroom to check on him because Anna was asleep or passed out, just lying there all ass-up on the bed in her white chonies. Miguel tried to wake her up, but she just moaned. So Miguel threw a pillow at her and told her to clean up the house and that the baby was crying and that we would be at Tiny's until late. Anna turned over, but she didn't open her eyes.

Even though she wasn't covering her tits, Anna was too nasty to look at. Her arms were all purple and her knees were like bottle caps on her legs. Her skinny, bony legs. She got uglier every day. When she first came around, she was hot and had cushion on her and the other guys were jealous of Miguel. I almost wanted to fuck her. But she turned into a skeleton and all she did was watch TV and eat Cheetos and yell at the baby to shut up. But Miguel kept her around and no one knew why. Maybe it was because he wouldn't let the baby go, the first grandson in the family. *Shit*, I'll never have a kid. Maybe it was because the State sent Anna money and if she left, Miguel would have to sell more or steal more or get a job. But that was going to end anyway. The government wasn't going to let someone like Anna keep a baby.

The apartment was fucked up. That's one of the problems with white girls, because no Mexican girl would let it get that nasty. Miguel told Anna, "It looks like shit in here," and Anna just said, "Then clean it up, asshole." And Miguel knew that if he hit her, she wouldn't even feel it, so he just called her *puta* and she turned back over. I said Miguel should kick Anna out and hook up with Tiny's cousin, Martha. But Miguel never listened to it, from me or anyone else. He was blinded by white snatch.

I said, "She's a worthless slut," and sprayed cologne onto my neck.

Miguel asked Anna, "Where's my knife?" but she didn't say anything. "Where the fuck is Guero's knife, *puta?*" Anna just laid there like a fucking junkie. The baby screamed louder, so Miguel left the bedroom and slammed the door.

The knife was from Guero, from when we caught that Salazar punk on 7th Street, a wannabe walking solo, carrying spraypaint and the knife. It was almost too easy. Guero was with me and Tiny, and that Salazar sewer rat barely put up a fight, helpless, like Guero was jumping him in or some shit, as if that *pinche* sureño would be let in. But he got red that day. Shit. When we were done with him, his shirt was purple.

Guero walked right up behind him, like he was going to step on his shoes, and that fool never noticed until it was too late, and Guero just said, "Hey *pendejo.*" And the Salazar kid looked back and saw Tiny and knew he was fucked, like it was over. And it was still afternoon so maybe he thought it was safe in the light, but borders don't change, day or night. Just the police patrols.

"You lost, *puto?*"

The Salazar shit tried to run but his pants hung past his shoes and he tripped over his own jeans. Stupid fucker. The knife fell out of his pocket. The spraypaint rolled to the curb. Guero stood over him like a lion. There was something that made Guero kick the shit out of the kid. I could feel it too. It was like the ancient Aztec blood in our veins and it made us warriors and it made me jump on that fucker's shoulders and it made Tiny kneel over him and jab at his jaw like a snake. And we beat the shit out of that *sur sissy* while he curled in a ball trying to cover his nuts.

I'm not saying there's nothing wrong with the jumps or the fights or the drivebys. In a better world, that shit wouldn't happen. But it's not a perfect world and it's not the gangs that fucked it up. We weren't even the first ones here. Maybe that shit happens because the cowboy motherfuckers, like Anna's brothers, don't act like real cowboys. They should keep scraps like the Salazars where they belong instead of driving around in their new shiny pickups. Those cowboys cruise around with their girlfriends, getting them pregnant and then paying for the abortions and then acting all good and shit. Anna told Miguel about how when she was still in school she had a cowboy boyfriend, and he was all into church and shit. That motherfucker got wasted on tequila, like he could drink tequila, then tried to fuck Anna in the *culo*. That's fucked up.

Miguel found the knife on the kitchen counter. He put it into his back pocket, in his jeans. He wore his jeans low, like they were held up by magic. He kept his herb in his front pocket. On the other side were six dollars in ones and his cheap-ass Wal-Mart phone. Miguel's shirt hung down to the knife. His hood, a sweatshirt I bought him at Target, sat on the kitchen counter with the car keys, with the dirty dishes, the cans of Pepsi, and the bags of Cheetos. Miguel grabbed the sweatshirt and the keys as I came out of the bathroom. Miguel yelled out to Anna that she better clean up. I just said, "Later, *puta*."

We got into Miguel's fucked-up Honda, some shitty Accord with bubbled tinting and flaking gold paint. Miguel started the car. He turned on the amp and stuck a CD into the stereo. "Old school," he said, and pumped the low end on the EQ.

It's all about the south side, brown pride, flowing through my veins.

"What's this shit?" I asked.

"It's good. Norteños can't rap," said Miguel.

"Fuck that shit," I said and spit the CD out, rolled down the window, and threw it in the street. "Put on some Sonny Boy." Miguel wanted to hit me, but he knew I was right. I said, "What if we get pulled over or shot listening to sureño shit?"

The music has to be right and the system has to be tight. Not like with the white boys and how they listen to country music through factory stereos. They roll down the windows in the summer and turn that shit up as loud as they can, like the music means something. But you can't feel music from stock sound. The white boys go to car races and get fucked up on Coors and then, maybe, they fight. But only on Fridays and Saturdays, like there's no war during the week. And it's only when somebody is drunk or fucking another guy's girlfriend. And they shake hands afterward, like it's a game.

Yakima used to be all whites and Yakamas, cowboys and Indians, like in those western movies. But those rodeo white boys aren't cowboys. They don't sleep under the stars unless they get drunk and pass out in an orchard. And the Indians don't fight. Yakamas were never warriors. They just stay down in the Valley by the river or the Casino. They put on their old feathers to march in parades and sell discount smokes. They didn't fight the cowboys back in the day, and they don't fight now. And the cowboys don't even give a fuck about the Indians unless they want to gamble or buy fireworks.

The gangs have to do everything. We need to be the cowboys *and* the Indians, the sheriffs and the tribes. And some people say we aren't any of those things, that we're just banditos. But that depends where you live. That Salazar *escrapa*. That pussy was a bandito. He crossed into territory that didn't belong to him. And Guero and Tiny and me were like old-west sheriffs. It's simple. Everyone knows the rules if they know anything. There aren't black hats and white hats or feathers. There are only red shirts and blue shirts. In Yakima, colors mean something. Colors show *familia*. They show borders.

◆

Miguel took the Yakima Avenue ramp. Fair Ave's quicker, but Miguel drove "The Ave" just to check the sidewalks for anybody who forgot where they belonged. The woofer shook the mirror. It filled the car. It vibrated some shitty Toyota in front. Miguel's car was ugly, but it drove smooth and the system was tight.

We used to talk about Yakima with some of the old timers, the old gangsters that had kids and went legit. This one guy named Victor (but they used to call him "Flaco" because he was skinny as shit) got all deep and he would talk about Yakima like it was a legend. He said how The Ave separated the real world and the dream world and that it used to be full of businesses and people who looked like they belonged in black-and-white movies. Those were the old days when it was *only* cowboys and Indians walking the streets, and they had a treaty so nobody fucked with anyone. Victor said that that Yakima died, but some people think it'll come back.

Back in the day, The Ave had the Mall, and I remember that because I used to steal shit from the Mervyn's and then get hot dogs at the Orange Julius. But the younger gangsters don't know any of that. Now there's a Convention Center and a hotel and potted plants, like somehow Yakima is safe for visitors.

Victor said all the work and government money didn't fix shit. He said how the buildings watched the change, that they could tell the story. "That's the real immigration," he said. "The people who used to live here, the ones with Buicks and Cadillacs, before rappers drove Escalades, are gone. They took their arts and crafts and Boy Scouts and camping trips and left. Now they live between Twenty-Fourth and Fortieth, between Tieton and Summitview. And those borders are shrinking."

Maybe Victor's right, because I can see it. Most of the rich whites went west to live near the orchards (where Anna's from) or north to the hills where the houses cost enough to keep Mexicans out. Now they shop in Union Gap at the Costco and the Old Navy during the day and go home at night.

Victor said the white people wouldn't come back to Yakima Avenue: "A hotel won't change shit, and turning the Bon into condos won't change shit."

Sometimes those people came downtown to the Capital Theatre, maybe, or the Olive Garden for prom nights and business lunches. But they don't live here. *We* live here now.

Everyone drives in and drives out. Nobody walks.

◆

Tiny's house was just off Naches. It was built back before the Mexicans started living in Yakima, when the migrants just passed through following the harvests. The whole neighborhood was old houses with wood floors and big rooms and hanging lights. We joked around about how if the people who built those houses could see them now, they'd shit and call the cops and say, "What are all these dirty Mexicans doing to my flowers?"

But Tiny could do whatever he wanted with his house. He could let it die. The neighborhood belonged to people like him, not like in those old pictures of Yakima, with white people in white shirts, wearing chinos like they're going to quinceañeras.

Tiny was like a gorilla and nobody messed with him, but he liked to fuck with the baby gangsters. He would make them drink until they passed out, then steal their money. He got the junior highers stoned and then he'd tell them, "Get me a hot dog from AM/PM, fucker." He left the younger ones alone if they brought girls to his house. He had drilled a hole in the bathroom wall so he could film the girls. Sick motherfucker.

Tiny was the storyteller. He told how he got arrested for possession, but then the judge let him go because the K-9 dog bit his throat. A lawyer helped him sue the cops, which is how he bought the house. Tiny went on about his brother who stabbed a Playboy in the eye and now he's a big OG in Walla Walla. Sometimes when Tiny was stoned he watched old Steven Segal movies and when some fool got blasted with a shotgun he shouted at the TV, "That shit's not real. They don't fly back. They just fall down." Then he'd tell some junior higher to get him a hot dog.

Miguel pulled up behind Tiny's car. Victor called that fucked-up green Hyundai a "hoopty." Everyone else just called it a piece of shit.

Albert's black Mazda was there, too. We hoped he left Angela, his girlfriend, at home. She's a half-Mexican/half-white girl who's pretty but talks too much. She has Albert whupped. She's the reason Jaime was still limping. Angela made Albert go to Shopko with her instead of backing Jaime. And Jaime was pissed, so he went to the Dollar Tree anyway, alone. A couple of CPV assholes saw him and beat him with a metal bar. Jaime was barely able to close the door and drive away. But those no-color chickenshits wouldn't have done it if Albert was there. Albert knew it was his fault, so he paid to fix the car. Then Albert and Jaime found those little Brown Pride *pendejos* and beat the shit out of them.

Back then, I was the only one who'd done any real time, so nobody gave me any shit. I spent sixteen months in State for breaking some wetback's jaw. I was fucked up and don't know why I went off on him. He wasn't even a gangster, just some *mojado* at Top Foods who bumped into me. Ever since, I've only done pot.

I got four months in county for breaking into hotels, but it was worth it. I brought one of the computers I took from the Fairfield to the parties. It had some insane shit on it, some thirty-year old redhead slut sticking a carrot up her snatch for her husband. Home movies. Every time I showed it, I'd say, "White people are fucked up" to mess with Miguel about Anna. Mostly, I liked showing that shit to the little punks that want to jump in. They worshipped us. They believed any shit we told them. They believed Tiny shot a cop. They believed *American*

Me was based on Jamie's dad. They didn't question anything. I showed them my appendix scar and said I was stabbed at Taco Bell. "*Órale*," they would say.

"Fuck yeah," I would say.

Miguel used to make up this shit about gangster life: "It's just like *The Godfather*. You have family and you have church and you don't betray that shit. But this is a fucked-up world and there's shit you have to do because you can't be some pussy and go to college and live off your dad's money," or some shit like that. Then he'd say, "You can't be some holy priest and act like nothing's fucked up. You have to work and you have to defend the family and you have to be loyal." I don't think he ever saw *Godfather*. He probably just got that shit from Victor.

Albert watched samurai movies so he told the new ones, "It's being a warrior. You have to know what you belong to and be bad-ass and watch your back 'cause there's always some fucker trying to take your land and rape your women." Angela rolled her eyes when Albert talked that shit.

◆

Miguel drank Pepsi and Bacardi while everyone else was still on Budweiser. The jump-in, some fat kid named Octavio, was trying some Budweiser to show he was tough, but it wasn't going down so Miguel made him a drink and handed him a joint. That *gordo* middle-schooler got buzzed quick. Maybe he thought if he was stoned, the jump-in wouldn't hurt. Jaime told him that even though Albert and Tiny were big, they held back. But Miguel told Octavio that I was a "vicious fucker." He said I jumped him in and broke two of his ribs. "My own fucking brother, *esé.*"

I took a drink and turned to the kid. "I'll just drink my beer and give you a few kicks. But if you make me spill, I'll beat you until blood comes out your ears."

Tiny came into the room wearing his "Bad-Ass Chef" apron and said the grill was lit. He asked Miguel where the burgers were, so Miguel shook his head. "Fuck," he said. That fool. He was all mad at me for taking so long and then he left the patties. All he had to do was remember the fucking burgers.

If Anna wasn't so worthless, she could have brought them. But Miguel knew she wasn't even awake, or if she was, she hadn't taken a shower or she was fucked up and he didn't want her at Tiny's or driving the baby around. So Miguel told me to go with him, but I didn't want to because I was showing Jaime pictures from one of the computers, this crazy old white dude wearing lipstick and a bra.

"Take Albert," I said.

"Shit. You know he has to stay here in case Angela needs him to go to Safeway and buy Kotex," he said.

"Fuck you," said Angela.

I drove because Miguel was already stoned and because no one was supposed to go anywhere alone.

"Take The Ave," said Miguel.

"Fuck The Ave," I said. "Fair's quicker."

When we got to the apartment, I dropped the seat back to stay in the car. I just wanted to get back to Tiny's, light up, and fuck up Octavio.

"C'mon Juan," he said. I told him he didn't need me to get burgers, but he was all scared.

"Fine," I said. "I have to take a shit anyway."

Anna was laying on the couch watching some home decorating show. The baby was sleeping by her so Miguel didn't yell. He just said, "Why watch this shit when you don't even care about your own house?" Anna didn't look at him or ask why he was home early. She just stared off at the screen and lifted her bruised right arm and flipped him off.

Puta.

The burgers were still on the counter, already buried under an empty Pepsi can and bunched-up paper towels, like Anna found a clean spot in the house and had to mess it up. Miguel grabbed the burgers and started telling Anna shit while I went to the bathroom. When I was in there, I heard the doorbell. The only people who rang doorbells were missionaries and police.

Then I heard Miguel walking down the hall and he knocked on the door.

"Hurry up, fucker," he said.

I was all, "I'm taking a shit," but Miguel didn't care.

The bell rang again and Miguel got nervous like he was a rat or something, and I heard him standing by the bathroom door, whispering to Anna, "Who is it?" But she didn't hear him or she didn't care, because she didn't say anything back.

Then the bell rang a third time, so Miguel started knocking on the door like he was tweaking, so I pinched off and said, "What the fuck?"

I opened the door and Miguel looked all crazy. He picked up a shoe from the bedroom and threw it at Anna. The shoe missed her and hit the baby and so he started crying. Anna was too wasted and thought the doorbell woke the baby. So she yelled at the door and asked who it was. I didn't know the voice and neither did Miguel, but it was a guy. Anna said, "What are you doing here?" and she was shouting, which made the baby cry louder. Miguel pushed us back into the bathroom and said, "What the fuck did you eat, nasty-ass motherfucker?" Then he went to the window above the bathroom like he was going to climb out.

I told him to calm down, but he wouldn't listen. He thought it was the cops, so I said, "Fuck the cops. They don't have any shit on you." He thought it was some sureños, and I said sewer rats don't ring doorbells.

Miguel was always crazy, but his head got fucked up after Guero was shot. He started talking about loyalty and protection and never went anywhere alone. He tipped his cup whenever he drank, whenever someone brought up Guero, like he was a trained dog. Sometimes I fucked with him and said how Guero was all *cholo*, so Miguel tipped his drink out of respect like he was making the sign of the cross or some shit. And then Tiny would get all pissed and yell at Miguel, "Hey motherfucker. You better clean that shit up."

I poked out the bathroom so I could hear Anna. She had opened the front door, but I couldn't tell what she was saying because the baby was too loud. Miguel thought about running, that he could get out of the window, so I said, "What would Guero think about you running?"

I was just trying to calm him down, but he got serious and quiet, like at a funeral. He reached to his back pocket and put his hand on Guero's knife. He said, "Guero wasn't scared of shit." He stepped off the bathtub and smoothed out his shirt. He looked in the mirror and made a head nod, like he was challenging himself to a battle.

"Who's out there?" he said as he slipped into the hallway.

"Shit, I don't know," I said. "Somebody that pissing Anna off 'cause she's going off."

"Is it cops?"

"How the fuck do I know?"

Miguel walked past me and to the end of the hallway. He slid one eye past the corner. It wasn't a direct shot of the door, but enough to see the front room.

"What are you doing?" yelled Anna at the door. "You don't belong here."

Miguel kept his ass against the wall and slid back to me. He whispered that he couldn't see a face, but he saw a cowboy boot holding the door open. He said, "It's probably that ass-fucker West Valley boyfriend trying to take Anna back."

"Let him," I said.

"Fuck you."

Miguel said he would sneak behind Anna and the couch and that he would bust through the door. He said he would take the cowboy, but that after he got through, I should follow him because there might be more than one. There's always more than one.

I moved to the corner while Miguel crawled across the floor. I couldn't see anything but I heard the white boy saying Anna needed to go with him. He said she needed to hurry and that they were going to be late.

Miguel crawled behind the couch, past the screaming baby. He walked in front of the TV and toward Anna and the door, and Anna didn't see him. She just kept telling the guy to go away.

Miguel got crazy, like he gets when he's high, like when he heard Guero got shot. He jumped to the door. He shoved Anna. He slammed her shoulder and she fell into the closet door, and she looked hurt bad, but she was too messed up to know what was going on. Then Miguel came out the door fast, like a boxer. He had his right hand on his back pocket, getting power from Guero's knife, so I chased after him and got to the door in three steps.

There were two of them, both dressed in cowboy boots and jeans and button-up shirts. Miguel got up into the little one's face, the one closest the door. He was all, "Who the fuck are you? What the fuck are you doing here, motherfucker?" The cowboy was still, like how people get around a growling pitbull.

I ran past them and to the big fucker, some football player that drank too much beer after high school. His belt buckle was a big gold circle with a bull on it and was almost covered by his gut. I could bring him down with one punch.

Miguel's eyes were red like his hood. His head jumped around, looking at the little one's chest and back to his eyes. Back and forth. Chest. Eyes. Chest. Eyes. Then he stayed locked in the eyes, like *El Mariachi*.

The little one stood on the edge of the porch and backed up in little steps. He tried to keep his eyes locked, but he looked down. Weak. He said he was there for Anna, which just made Miguel more pissed, so Miguel stepped closer to the cowboy. There wasn't any air between them and the little one knew he was fucked, but he couldn't do anything. I stayed with the big one in case he tried to help. The fat asshole looked over his shoulder and turned sideways, so I moved with him, keeping between him and the little one. Part of me wanted them to run away so we could get back to Tiny's. The rest of me wanted the cowboys to be stupid.

The little one looked to the door as Anna stood up. Dumb-ass mistake. Miguel raised his hands and shoved the fucker in the chest and that *pendejo* fell off the porch onto grass and rocks. "You looking at my girl, fucker? You want to fuck her in the ass, *maricón?*"

Anna screamed for Miguel to stop, but he reached into his pocket and pulled out Guero's knife. He looked at Anna and told her to shut the fuck up and "go in and take care of the baby, *puta.*" And Anna yelled louder, so I shoved the big one, because this was about to start, and I closed in on him, chest to chest, like Miguel and his cowboy.

The white boys were smart enough to know they had nothing. The big one didn't say shit. He stared all angry, but he wasn't a fighter. The little one lifted himself off the rocks, but Miguel stood over him like how Guero covered that Salazar *escrapa.* The little one just crawled back, stood, and didn't say a word to Anna. He didn't look at her. The fuckers walked backwards as we followed them. Miguel moved his head back and forth like a cobra looking for a place to strike. Chest to chest. The white boys put their hands up like we were police. I've seen some crazy shit.

The little one followed Miguel's knife hand as Anna screamed. By now the apartment doors were opening and the whole complex was watching. Some little kid shouted for Miguel to stab the cowboys. Anna yelled that she would call the police. That slut probably would.

When we reached the grass in front of the next apartment,

Miguel let space come between him and the cowboy. So I let the fat one go. The cowboys backed toward a red pickup and I wondered if the color was a sign of something. Maybe that's why they got to walk away. They got in the truck. They drove away and we stood still because sometimes that's the only way to handle the fire inside.

Anna screamed how much she hated us, and Miguel just shouted back, "*Cállate*," and told her to go in and take care of the baby. And Anna said, "Those are my brothers you assholes."

The apartment doors closed as people went back inside.

Miguel said he would grab the burgers and that we should get back to Tiny's before the police showed. I went to the Honda while Miguel walked back to the apartment door, but Anna, that junkie, had locked it. Miguel pounded on the door and told Anna to open it because his keys were still in the bathroom, but she just told him to fuck off.

I heard the car first. Maybe if I had my gun, but that was under the seat, and that wouldn't have opened the door for Miguel. The car drove too fast for the apartments. The windows were tinted, but it didn't matter. I knew what was inside. Some fucker had a blue bandana wrapped around his mouth and leaned out the window with both hands on an automatic. I yelled to Miguel and ran to the Honda, but I was too slow. Fire went through my leg and I couldn't stand. I rolled away from the road.

Miguel was stone. He was loyal and so he wanted to run to me, but he couldn't. So he stood there. I watched that fucking car close in, the primer-coated Corolla, and I thought how Victor said all the good cars were gone. "Whatever happened to El Dorados, Monte Carlos, Impalas? Back in the day, no gangster would get caught driving some Japanese shit."

Miguel held Guero's knife in front of him, like one of Albert's samurais, like it could block bullets.

It was like Tiny said. There was no jump back, no fall through a window. Miguel's body just stopped working, like a puppet with the strings cut, and he fell. He dropped Guero's knife and he landed on the rocks where the cowboy fell. He didn't move. He just laid there like a shirt.

The pain in my leg went away. I could feel the Aztec blood flowing. I pulled my dead leg to the car and opened the door and reached under the seat. The Corolla stopped across the road and one of those fuckers shouted, "Fuck ass *norcacas*," and "Get the knife."

I pulled the slide back and hoped the gun was loaded and fired at the fucker on the ground by Miguel. But I aimed high because I didn't want to hit Miguel. The sureño jumped into the car and those pussies ran off, and I couldn't squeeze the trigger anymore, but Guero's knife stayed with Miguel.

I saw Anna, and she was standing by Miguel and then she jumped off the porch and fell onto Miguel's body and screamed. She let out all the anger and hate and fear that I had, but couldn't show. I hated her and I hated Miguel and the stupid, fucking town. I tried to pull my body to Miguel but I couldn't reach him. And then there was quiet and my ears stopped and I was warm and cold and I looked and the last thing I saw was color.

DON'T ASK
37TH ST AND MOUNTAINVIEW

Thanksgiving is in Seattle this year (with Katy's parents). Jill will feed the assumption, saying Katy "is the smartest, kindest, most beautiful woman she's ever known." Katy will echo it at Christmas (in Yakima with Jill's parents). And on New Year's Eve, free of family, Jill and Katy will compare notes about their relationships and wish they didn't love men.

ACKNOWLEDGMENTS

"Arrivals and Departures" appeared in the 2016 edition of *DoveTales*.

"Don't Ask" appeared in the April 2015 edition of *Flash: The International Short-Short Story Magazine*.

"First Day" appeared in the Winter 2015 edition of *Mused*.

"Persona, or All Sanctuaries Smell Like Stockholm" appeared in the Spring 2016 edition of the *Santa Clara Review*.

"Starlings" won the Editor's Choice award and appeared in the Fall 2012 edition of *Carve Magazine*.

ABOUT THE AUTHOR

Joe Johnson writes fiction, poetry, and nonfiction. His work has appeared in *Flash*, *Heron Tree*, *Rust+Moth*, *Aethlon*, and *The Santa Clara Review*, among others. He has won the Editor's Choice Award for *Carve Magazine* and was a finalist for *Fiction Southeast*'s Ernest Hemingway Flash Fiction Prize and for the Ruby Irene Poetry Chapbook Contest. He is a graduate of the Rainier Writing Workshop at Pacific Lutheran University and lives in Portland, Oregon, with his family.